Swingerz

By Patricia M. Goins

Other Books by Patricia M. Goins

www.patriciagoinsbooks.com

Essence The Poetry Of Life

This Can't Be Love

The Love House

Ladies Delight

Are You Ready To Open Your Gifts From God?

SWINGERZ

The Symbol

This is a work of fiction. All of the characters, organizations, and events portrayed in this novel are either products of the author's imagination or are used fictitiously.

Swingerz

Author's Note

I'd like to acknowledge and thank Café Mom members of the Erotica Stories Group: Cocobrin, Larschick, Rainbow_mommy09, Tigeroo, WordsPlayToday, Edaley, Dollnh, and Kathystoll for their postings and suggestions to the storyline while I was writing this book online. If you're looking for a wonderful social media site for moms, I would definitely recommend www.cafemom.com.

I want to thank my children Aaron, Ebony, Isaiah, and Joshua for being so patient with their mom and loving me unconditionally. I want to thank all the friends and family who have encouraged me along the way. I also want to thank all my readers who support my dream by purchasing and reading my books.

Special thanks to my sister Angela E. Stevenson and her company AES Productions, for assisting me in bringing this story to life. I want to also give a special thanks to my little sister Nicole Goins-Turner for always having my back. I love you more than I can ever put into words.

Most importantly, I want to thank God blessing me with this creative gift, and for never giving up on me, even in my imperfection. For always loving me and guiding my footsteps and holding me up during the times I didn't feel like I could do it myself.

Chapter 1

“I can't believe I'm actually going through with this,” Leslie whispered out loud as she waited in the truck while her husband locked the front door. “A swingers club? I must be losing my mind,” she said to herself as she opened the sun visor, inspecting her makeup in the mirror.

Leslie promised Ed she’d do whatever it took to save their marriage. She had dealt with his infidelity for years. Right when the flame of one affair had finally settled down, it seemed like another one was in the fire. The thought of leaving him was just inconceivable. Ed was everything she dreamed her husband would be when she was growing up. He was so handsome with his curly black hair and cute dimples. His sexy body showed evidence of years of eating healthy, exercise, and lifting weights. He was also a very intelligent man. A law graduate of Harvard, he'd been in the top five percent of his class. His father, a well-known lawyer, promised to turn the prosperous family law firm over to his only son upon his death.

They started dating in middle school. She sometimes wondered what Ed had seen in her. She had been such a nerd and an introvert back then. Opposite from Ed, who was the honor student and popular athlete. All the girls loved him. There were rumors in high school of his cheating ways, but Leslie had been too much in love to give the rumors any serious thought. She figured the girls were just jealous that he had chosen her instead of them. Leslie loved her husband deeply. He always went out of his way to make her feel special. He continuously showered her with affection, expensive gifts, and vacations. Not to mention the sex was still amazing after eight years of marriage.

The only problem was he just couldn't seem to stay faithful. After the last girl he had an affair with tried to kill Leslie by running her over with her car, Ed had finally agreed to go to marriage counseling. A lot came out in those counseling sessions. One major secret her husband had kept from her was his sexual addiction. He revealed that he'd been held captive to this addiction ever since his teenage years. Leslie began to feel sorry for him. So after years of battling to keep her husband for herself, Leslie finally decided to give in. She was desperate and willing to do almost anything to keep her marriage together. Against her better judgment, Leslie agreed to go to a swinger's club with her husband. Ed assured her that if Leslie was with him, it couldn't be considered cheating.

"You ready to go baby?" Ed asked with a smile on his face as he got into the driver's side of the white Chevy Blazer and placed a gentle kiss on her cheek. Leslie shook her head yes. The touch of his soft lips on her face still sent chills up her spine. She was so attracted to him. If only he could have eyes just for her.

By the time they reached Tiger's, a popular swinging nightclub in Atlanta, Leslie's stomach was doing somersaults. The parking lot was packed. After finally finding a parking space, Ed got out and walked around the truck, opening the passenger door and holding out his hand to his wife. Leslie gave him a nervous smile as she placed her hand in his and got out of the truck.

"You look so beautiful tonight. " Ed said, smiling as he placed a soft kiss on her lips.

"Thank you baby," Leslie replied.

Leslie noticed other couples walking towards the entrance of the building, she wondered if any of the women felt as uncomfortable and out of place as she did. When they entered the building, Leslie was surprised at how crowded it was. The room was filled with couples dancing and mingling. Some of the couples were leaning against mirrored walls, while others were standing around a large white-water fountain in the middle of the room that had two naked statues embraced in a kiss. Leslie followed Ed across the waxed hardwood floors towards an unoccupied red leather couch, that sat against a mirrored wall.

"Have a seat baby I'll be right back. I'm going to get us a drink." Ed said pointing towards the couch before walking off toward the large glass bar on the opposite side of the room. As Leslie sat down on the couch, she glanced around the room. She couldn't help but stare at some of the couples taking turns engaging in passionate kisses with each other's partner. Leslie tore her gaze away from one of the couples when Ed walked back over to her and handed her a Margarita with a salt rim and splash of strawberry juice. The soft jazz music blasting through the club's sound system was very relaxing.

After drinking the Margarita, Leslie began to feel a little more at ease. Ed helped her take off her jacket, revealing a sexy red button-down dress that hugged her curves and caught the attention of almost every man and woman in the room. Ed smiled as he led her to the dance floor as eyes gawked at them.

"I'm glad you're starting to relax baby," Ed whispered in her ear as he pulled her close to him. They began swaying their bodies to the rhythm of the music.

"I guess the drink helped a lot," Leslie giggled. Once the song ended, Ed guided Leslie back over to the couch and then walked back to the bar to get them another drink. When Ed returned, he was accompanied by a man and a woman.

"This is my lovely wife Leslie," Ed said proudly as he handed Leslie her drink.

"Hi Leslie, my name is Mia and this is my husband, Chris."

"Nice to meet you Leslie," Chris said in a sexy deep voice as he leaned across the table and held out his hand. Leslie tried to ignore the way Chris was staring at her cleavage. He was very handsome in a rugged type of way. He had an attractive face and well-groomed beard. His tall, muscular frame seemed to demand attention.

"It's nice to meet both of you," Leslie replied as she leaned forward and shook both Chris and Mia's hand, before sitting back against the couch pillows and taking a sip of her Margarita.

Leslie began to feel nervous again. Mia is so beautiful, Leslie thought to herself as she stared at Mia's oval shaped face, voluptuous breast, tiny waist, and curvy hips. How could I possibly compete with her? Is this the woman Ed wants to sleep with tonight? Jealousy took a stab at her heart, but then was quickly replaced with worry. What if he falls in love with her? Leslie thought to herself. She couldn't help but notice that Mia's husband was staring at her like he wanted to tear Leslie's dress off and make love to her right there on the couch in front of everyone. Leslie tried her best to ignore his penetrating gaze. Am I supposed to have sex with him? I don't think I can go through with this? She mumbled to herself, taking another sip of her Margarita. Just as quick as the thought of backing out entered her mind, she began feeling guilty. She made a promise to Ed that she would do whatever it took to save their marriage. She couldn't break her promise. She knew the only way she would be able to get through this was to keep reminding herself of that promise.

After an hour of small talk, the two couples decided to leave Tiger's and continue a private party of their own at Leslie and Ed's house. Once they reached their house, and after a few shots of Tequila, Mia started things off. She walked over to Leslie and began kissing her on her ruby red covered lips, as she massaged Leslie's breast with her petite hands. Leslie was surprised by how turned on she was by this beautiful woman. After their kiss ended, Chris walked over to Leslie and Mia. He kissed Mia before pulling Leslie into his arms. He began kissing her as Mia walked over to Ed and began massaging his manhood.

After several minutes of a lusty make out session, Ed led Mia to one of the many guest rooms. Leslie watched as Mia and Ed disappeared into one of the rooms before awkwardly leading Chris to a guest room on the opposite side of the house. Leslie made Ed promise that their marriage bed would remain sacred.

Once in the guest room Chris looked at Leslie and smiled. Leslie quickly sat down on the bed, placing her hands on her lap, and began twirling her thumbs. She couldn't seem to calm her nerves. All kinds of crazy thoughts were running through her mind. What would her mother say if she knew her daughter was about to have sex with a man she didn’t know and who wasn't her husband, while Ed was in another room with another woman? Chris interrupted her thoughts when he walked over to her and sat down next to her on the bed.

"This is your first time isn't it?" He asked gently.

"Yes, how can you tell?" Leslie whispered nervously.

"I've been doing this for a long time. I can always spot out swinging virgins," Chris chuckled. He leaned over and placed soft kisses on her neck. With each kiss, Leslie scooted away from him just a little. When he put his fingers on the first button of her dress, Leslie quickly placed her hand over his to stop his fingers from moving.

"What's wrong?" He asked with a concerned look on his face.

"I don't think I can go through with this. I mean you're a very handsome man, but this just isn't me," Leslie whispered.

"There's nothing to be afraid of. I promise I won't hurt you," Chris whispered as he removed her hand and began playing with her breast through her dress, causing her nipples to grow erect.

"I'm sorry but I just can't go through with this!" She yelled as she jumped off the bed and headed towards the door.

"Hey, wait a minute," Chris replied as he jumped up from the bed and followed her, reaching the door just before she had a chance to turn the door knob. He placed his hand flat against the door to keep it from opening. This made Leslie feel even more uneasy, was he going to rape her? Suddenly fear crept in.

Chris could feel Leslie's rising anxiety, he removed his hand from the door and stepped back. As soon as Leslie opened the bedroom door, they both heard the loud sounds of lovemaking from the other guest bedroom. Leslie felt her face turn warm from embarrassment. Then shame and hurt set in as she lowered her head. The sounds of her husband making love to another woman seemed to tear her heart apart. She began crying.

"Listen, I've never raped a woman before in my life, and I don't plan on starting tonight. You want to sit down and talk?" He asked as he walked back over to the bed and sat down. Chris couldn't believe he was saying these words. Things were not going as he had planned. He was supposed to be in the middle of a heated fucking session, not consoling Ed's emotional wife.

Leslie began to feel a little more at ease with Chris. She walked back over to a chair that was across from the bed and sat down as she wiped the tears from her eyes, taking a deep breath. When she heard her husband let out another loud moan, she knew she wasn't going to be able to deal with what she was hearing.

"Can you please take me away from here?" She whispered as she searched for her purse. Once she found it on the floor, she picked it up and began searching inside. She pulled out a set of car keys and a tissue and wiped her face.

"What about your husband?"

"Can't you hear them? He's busy!" She replied sarcastically.

"Oh yea, they are getting it in," Chris chuckled.

"I don't see anything funny! He's in there with your wife, don't you even care?" She asked with raised eyebrows.

"Mia's not really my wife. She's just a close friend and business partner. Mia and I enjoy role playing. I would never share my wife with another man," Chris shrugged. As soon as the words escaped from his lips, he wanted to pull them back in. It was obvious that last sentence hit her below the belt.

"Please just take me somewhere. I can't bear the thought of being here right now." Leslie whispered as she stood up and walked out the room. When they both stepped into the hallway, Chris slowly closed the bedroom door behind him.

"You want to take a walk?" He asked.

"Sure, that's fine," Leslie sighed. Leslie led the way to the front door. It still felt warm outside. The moon seemed so bright.

"Why did you even go to a swinger's club? Why are you doing this if this isn't what you really want to do?"

"I was trying to save my marriage," Leslie replied sarcastically as she wrapped her arms around her body in response to a sudden breeze that made her hair bounce in the wind.

"If you have to go through all this to save a marriage, is it really worth it?"

"Yes, to me it is. I grew up with parents who've been married for thirty years. Divorce is not something we do. Plus, I love my husband," Leslie whispered as a single tear slide down her cheek. Chris stopped walking and pulled her toward him. He wiped away the tear that had almost made its way to her top lip and looked deep into her eyes.

"So instead you let him sleep with other women? If you were my wife, I wouldn't share you with anyone." Chris pulled her close to him, molding his body against hers. Leslie could feel his hard manhood pressing against her. This time she didn't pull away as Chris began kissing her. His tongue made small circles around her lips before entering her mouth. An unexplainable emotion shot through Leslie that she'd never felt for anyone else except Ed. She felt a deep sensual feeling as their tongues intertwined.

"Hey, why are you two out here!" Leslie and

Chris jerked apart and quickly turned around to see Ed standing in the middle of the driveway wearing a black silk robe and an angry look on his face.

Chapter 2

There was something about seeing his wife cuddled up and kissing another man outside in the moonlight that Ed didn't like. Sure, he’d given her permission to sleep with someone else, and yes, this was a swinging date, but Ed knew Leslie wasn't really going to go through with it. He had expected Leslie to come barging into the room, catching him in the middle of fucking Mia, and cause a dramatic scene. He had expected to hear her ranting and raving about him not being loyal! The thought of his wife walking in and catching him fucking the shit out of another woman turned him on. It had always been one of his secret sexual fantasies. He had kept his eye on the bedroom door as he twisted Mia around on the bed, allowing him to get it doggy style. He wanted to make sure Leslie was able to get a good view. But after thirty minutes of fucking and making loud noises, Ed realized that his wife wasn’t going to barge into the room and decided it was time to investigate.

Regardless of what people who knew their situation thought, Ed truly loved Leslie. He never had any real feelings for the women he had sex with. To him, they were just human objects used to fulfill his sexual fantasies. After the sex act, he was ready to leave the dream world and return to his loving wife.

He probably should've felt a little guilty for abruptly getting up in the middle of sex and walking out on Mia. He could hear her asking what was wrong and begging him to return to the bed as he walked toward the door, but he blocked her out as he left the room and made his way to the other guest room. His only thought was finding his wife. His heart was beating like drums against his chest as his hand reached for the door knob. What if she really did sleep with Mia's husband? Fear set in as he turned the doorknob. When he realized the room was empty, and the bed was still neatly made, he let out a sigh of relief. Thank God, she hadn't gone through with it, but deep inside he knew she wouldn't. He'd known Leslie since the 8th grade. He knew what she would and wouldn't do. He knew that she didn't want to swing. But he also knew that Leslie believed the only way to keep women out of her husband's bed when she wasn't around, was to agree to hook up with other swingers.

He began to feel nervous. Where could they have gone? What if the guy was a killer or a rapist? Had he kidnapped his wife? Ed knew that swinging was risky. He didn't know much about Chris. Ed had just met him a few weeks earlier through a client his law firm was representing.

Ed's pulse began to race as he ran outside and saw their cars still parked in the driveway. He quickly walked down to the middle of the driveway ready to pull out his cell phone and dial 911 when he saw them kissing. His heart dropped. What the fuck was this guy doing kissing his wife! He yelled out to them again, this time with a little more anger in his voice.

"What the fuck are the two of you doing out here!" Ed screamed again as his eyes narrowed in on Chris.

"We came out here because I didn't feel like listening to my husband fuck another woman. I'm ready for this to be over Ed!" Leslie yelled. She briefly glanced at Chris before walking toward the house.

"Well you heard my wife, it's time for you two to leave!" Ed demanded. Chris didn't say anything. He gave Ed the evilest look before walking toward his car. When he reached the end of the driveway, Mia came outside completely dressed.

"I'm ready to leave Chris! Can you believe this jerk left all this in bed alone? No one walks out on me!" Mia yelled pointing at her curves before jumping in the passenger side of Chris's car. Chris didn't say anything. He glanced in the direction of the guest bedroom window. He caught a glimpse of Leslie peeking through the blinds. When Leslie realized she had been spotted she quickly closed the blinds.

"What's taking you so long to get off my property!" Ed yelled.

"Hey man, chill. We're leaving!" Chris yelled back as he got into the car. At that moment, Chris decided that Leslie was going to be his by any means necessary. He gave Ed one last long stare before pulling out of his driveway and driving away. Mia was ranting and raving about how pissed she was at how the night turned out. Chris wasn’t paying her any attention. His mind was too busy working on a plan.

Leslie watched Chris and Mia drive away. She turned away from the window and walked into the living room, sitting down on the couch. Why was his kiss still engraved in her memory? She asked herself. She could still remember the tingling sensation she felt when Chris kissed her. Her thoughts were interrupted as Ed walked into the house.

"Why were you outside kissing that guy? You want our neighbors to start spreading rumors about us? You know how nosey Ms. Jefferson is. Why were the two of you outside anyway?"

"I was upset about you sleeping with that woman. I wanted to get away. He suggested we take a walk. He just happened to kiss me. It was no big deal. I can't believe I 'm even explaining myself to you when you were in there doing God knows what to that woman. Ed, I love you, but if swinging is the only way I can save this marriage, then we might as well file for a divorce right now. I will not do this again!" Leslie declared as she stood up, putting her hands on her hips. Ed walked over to her and placed a soft kiss on her forehead.

"Don't worry baby, we won't do it again. Now, let's put icing on tonight's cake by making love, I have a taste for some of your sweet crème," he whispered as he began running his fingers through her hair. Leslie pushed his hand away and walked away from him. A look of disgust covered her face.

"I know you don't really think I'm going to let you touch me after being with another woman just thirty minutes ago," she said frowning.

"I'm sleeping in the guest room tonight Ed, Goodnight!" She brushed past him and walked out of the room.

"She'll be alright tomorrow," Ed said shrugging his shoulders. He pulled out the business card Mia had given him and smiled. He made a mental note to send Mia a bouquet of roses to her job. She was pretty good in the bed and she was very good with her mouth. He would have to keep her around. He put the card back in his pocket and walked into the kitchen to pour himself a shot of Tequila before going to bed.

Leslie ran to the guest room as fast as her feet would carry her and slammed the door so hard she thought it might come off the hinges. She locked the door, sank to her knees, and cried.

"How can he continue to do this to me over and over again? Doesn't he care about my feelings at all?" She screamed out loud through her tears. All the sudden her thoughts turned to Chris. Now there's a man that cares she thought. Something snapped inside Leslie and she knew she had to find Chris. She picked up her purse and crept out the back door. Leslie drove back to Tiger's, hoping that Chris and Mia would have gone back there looking for another couple after tonight's fiasco. After an hour of waiting, no sign of Chris or Mia, and numerous advances from other couples, Leslie left the club with her hopes dashed. She didn't know exactly what she was hoping for, but she knew she had to thank him for being so kind to her.

"Oh well, it was a long shot anyway," she mumbled to herself. Not ready to go home just yet, Leslie decided to stop at a neighborhood pub near her home and have a drink. She went up to the bar and was about to order when she felt a pair of eyes on her. She turned around to see who it was. Low and behold, not ten feet away from her stood the very man she'd been searching for.

Chris walked toward her smiling. He had such a sexy smile. Leslie felt herself grow warm all over as he approached her.

"I thought you and your husband were in for the night," he said as he sat down on a bar stool next to her and placed his beer on the counter.

"He uh well uh," Leslie stuttered.

"Cat got your tongue?" Chris laughed.

"No, actually I kind of snuck out. I came out looking for you. I wanted to apologize to you and Mia. Where is she?" Leslie asked as the bartender handed her a Bloody Mary. Leslie reached into her purse to pull out her money, but Chris placed his hand over hers. When she looked up at him, he shook his head.

"I'll pay for it," he said as he handed the bartender a twenty-dollar bill.

"Thanks," Leslie said as she began stirring her drink.

"To answer your question, I dropped Mia off at her house. I couldn't sleep so I decided to come back out and have a drink. No need to apologize about tonight. I understand," he said smiling.

"My husband can be kind of rude and obnoxious sometimes."

"You're such a beautiful woman. I don't understand how your husband could want to be with anyone else but you."

"I guess I'm not enough woman for him. I've been dealing with his cheating ways for years. At first, I thought if I tried harder to be a better wife, tried to look sexier, or have sex whenever and however he wanted it, that he'd stop sleeping around with other women. But no matter what I did to try to please him, he continued to have affairs. I've been begging him for years to go to counseling, but he kept saying we didn't need it. When one of his bitches tried to run me over with her car a couple of months ago, I guess he saw the seriousness of the situation, because he finally agreed to go to marriage counseling." She shrugged as she took a sip of her drink.

"Well, if the two of you decided to go to counseling and work on your marriage, why in the world were you guys at a swinger's club?" He asked as he picked up his beer and took a drink.

"I found out he has a sexual addiction. So, I agreed to do whatever was necessary to save our marriage. I figured if I allowed him to swing every once in a while, that it would keep him from sneaking around behind my back. I didn't know what else to do. I love him," Leslie whispered. She felt so ashamed and hurt. She couldn't believe she was telling all this to an absolute stranger. She wasn't the type to talk about her private business with other people. But there was something about Chris that made her feel comfortable and safe.

"Hey, why don't we go somewhere we can talk privately, it's too noisy in here," Chris said as he took another drink of his beer.

"No, I'm sorry but I can't. Ed doesn't even know I left the house," Leslie said as she glanced at her watch before standing up.

"Well can I at least treat you to lunch tomorrow?" Chris asked. He was determined that he wasn't going to let her get away from him.

"Sure, here's my card, just give me a call before 1pm. I work downtown and usually take lunch around 1," she said as she reached into her purse, pulled out a business card, and handed it to him.

"London Care Medical Associates, what do you do there?" He asked as he read the card before putting it in his pocket.

"I'm a Cardiology Nurse." She said as she took one last drink from her glass before picking up her purse.

"At least allow me to walk you out to your car," Chris said as he stood up. Leslie was caught off guard when he took hold of her hand and led her out of the bar. Even though, she knew someone could have easily recognized her and told Ed that she was holding hands with another man, for some reason she didn't care. When they reached her car, she pulled out her keys and unlocked her door.

"I'll see you tomorrow," He said as she got into the car and put the key into the ignition.

"Okay," Leslie replied before closing the door and pulling out of the parking lot. Leslie glanced in the rear-view mirror and realized that he was still standing there watching her drive away. What was she doing? Had she just agreed to meet Chris again? Leslie asked herself as she drove home.

The next morning Leslie was awakened by her husband's kisses. He was lying next to her in the bed butt naked. She wanted to push him away because she was still mad at him about last night.

But she didn't want to do anything that would give him an excuse to turn to another woman. Ed sucked on her lower lip before trailing kisses to her ear. He continued to nibble on her earlobe before allowing his tongue to take a quick journey into her ear and then continuing his journey down her neck. He took his time sucking on her neck until he saw the area turn red. Then repositioned himself, straddling her legs as he pulled off her gown. He trailed kisses down to her breast. Taking time to circle each nipple with his tongue before putting each nipple in his mouth and sucking on them like he was a newborn baby searching for milk. Leslie moaned as she watched him devour her breast. She slowly moved her hand down to her womanhood, her fingers searching for her clitoris. Once her fingertip felt the top of her clitoris, she began massaging it as she continued to watch her husband devour her breast like it was his last meal. When he saw the motion of her hand, he quickly abandoned her breast and allowed his kisses to follow the path to her hand. He lowered his body between her legs and moved her hand out of the way. He kissed both lips before allowing his tongue to replace where her fingers had been. Leslie moaned as his tongue began massaging her clitoris. He moved his hands back up to her breast and began to massage her nipples as his tongue took a deeper journey into her womanhood and began licking and sucking her juices into his mouth. Leslie began to draw her legs up toward her chest as a familiar warmth began to spread throughout her body. With each movement of his tongue, her body seemed to grow more and more tense until finally, the floodgates opened. She screamed as a hard orgasm shook her body.

"That's right baby, give it all to me," he moaned. Before her orgasm subsided, Ed quickly mounted her like a stallion. He wanted to feel the vibrations of her orgasm against his manhood. He plunged in letting out a loud moan as the warmth and wetness of her womanliness surrounded him, holding him hostage as he began moving in and out. He started slow, expertly aiming each stroke, going deeper and deeper. After about thirty minutes of slow grooving he decided to change positions. He loved making love to his wife from the back. Her voluptuous curves turned him on. He flipped her onto her stomach and pulled her halfway off the bed causing her legs to dangle from the bed before reentering her from the back. Leslie moaned; she knew that he was about to beat her pussy like it stole something. The sound of his hand smacking her buttocks could be heard in the silence of the early morning as he went deep and fast.

"Oh my, baby, this feels so good. This is all mine. All mine. Give it to me baby, lift your butt up so I can get to the center of the tootsie roll pop," he yelled as he went deeper and faster. Just when Leslie thought she couldn't take anymore, Ed let out a loud scream before collapsing onto her back. After a few seconds, he plopped down on the bed and kissed her on the back of her neck.

"I love you baby," Ed whispered in her ear.

"I love you too," she replied. Ed stood up and walked out of the guest room without bothering to put his pajama pants back on. Leslie continued to lie in the bed still exhausted from the early morning workout. If only she didn't love him so much. She thought to herself. She finally pulled herself out of the bed, put on her robe and walked out of the bedroom and up the stairs. She could hear the shower running in their master bathroom. Leslie walked into the bathroom, took off her robe, and joined her husband in the shower. She picked up the soap and cloth and began washing his back. When Ed turned around his manhood was standing at full attention. Ed turned his wife around in the shower and entered her from the back, picking up where he'd left off in the guest room. Leslie moaned as Ed tried to hit every nook and cranny before finally releasing. Then he picked up the washcloth and took his time washing the evidence of their lovemaking from in between her legs before getting out of the shower. Leslie continued washing up before turning off the shower. She picked up a towel off the rack and dried herself before putting her robe back on.

Leslie walked downstairs to the kitchen and began making breakfast. Twenty minutes later, Ed walked into the kitchen completely dressed in his business suit just as Leslie was making his plate. He sat down at the kitchen table as Leslie placed a plate with eggs, bacon, toast, and grits in front of him.

"Hey baby, I have to work late tonight so don't worry about cooking dinner. We're about to take the O'Connor case to trial, so all the partners are pulling a late night," Ed said as he put a fork full of eggs in his mouth.

"Do you want me to bring something to the office for you this evening?" Leslie asked as she placed a cup of coffee in front of him?"

"No, we'll probably just order something," Ed replied. After breakfast, Ed kissed Leslie before heading out the door. Once he pulled his car out of the driveway he drove to the next block before pulling over. He pulled Mia's business card out of his pocket. Then pulled out his cell phone and dialed the florist.

"Hello, this is Edward Johnson Jr, I would like a dozen red roses sent to 1223 Marietta St Atlanta, Georgia suite 123. For Ms. Mia Anderson. Please include a card that says; I'm sorry about last night. Let's have dinner tonight so I can make up for yesterday. I'll pick you up at 6pm. And sign it; Sincerely Ed." He repeated the message twice for the florist. "Please use the credit card on file. I want the roses sent this morning." Ed said before putting the card back in his pocket and pulling back onto the street.

"No problem Mr. Johnson, the roses should be delivered by 10:30 this morning," the clerk replied.

"Excellent," Ed said pushing the red end button on his cellphone. He couldn't wait to feel Mia's lips on his dick, he thought to himself as he drove his car onto the I- 20West ramp.

Chapter 3

When Mia received the flowers, she smiled to herself. She dialed Ed's home number and asked to speak with Leslie. Leslie was very sweet and understanding. Leslie agreed to have dinner at Mia's house that night. Mia then called Ed and invited him over to her house an hour after Leslie was to arrive. Mia worked hard on the meal. When Leslie arrived, they shared a bottle of wine, and ate dinner. The food was delicious. After dinner, they settled on the living room couch and Mia began telling Leslie about her swinging lifestyle. She told her how much she enjoyed being with the woman more than the man. Mia loved watching Leslie blush. Mia excused herself and called Ed to tell him she was running behind at work and that she would leave the back door unlocked so he could let himself in. When she got back to the living room, she walked up to the couch, got on her knees, pushed Leslie's panties aside, and put her head in between Leslie's legs. She started kissing and licking Leslie's womanhood. Leslie let out a loud moan as she threw her head back against the couch pillows. Ed walked into the living room and smiled as he began unzipping his pants as he watched Mia and Leslie...

"Mr. Johnson, Mr. Johnson..." The receptionist said as she shook Ed awake. Ed jumped up, using the sleeve of his jacket to wipe the saliva from the side of his mouth. He looked around the room with wide eyes, relaxing once he realized he was still at work and not at Mia's house. He didn't remember falling asleep. That's what he got for staying up late on a work night, he thought to himself as he straightened his neck tie. His lack of sleep was finally catching up with him.

"I'm so sorry to wake you sir but you have a call holding on line 3," the receptionist said before walking out the office, gently closing the door behind her.

Wow, what a dream Ed said to himself. His precious wife cheating on him with Mia? Them having a threesome, he could feel the rise in his pants. Ed picked up the phone and hit button three on the phone.

"Edward Johnson Jr speaking, how may I help you?"

"Hello Ed, it's Mia, I just wanted to thank you for the roses. I also got your message about dinner. Would you like for me to come over to your house for dinner this evening?"

"Ah, no, uh, well, uh...how about we meet at Smokey's on Tara Blvd," Ed stuttered.

"I think I know where it is. Sure, that's fine. But I don't get off work until 6pm so how about we meet around 7:30?" She asked.

"Yes, that's fine," Ed replied.

"Okay see you tonight," Mia said before ending the call. After hanging up the phone, Ed leaned back in his chair, interlocking his fingers behind his head, and smiled.

"Okay Mrs. Davidson, can you please raise up your sleeve, so I can check your blood pressure?" Leslie asked the elderly patient.

"Sure Suga, I think it might be up a little today. I probably shouldn't have eaten those fried pork chops last night." Mrs. Davidson said as she began rolling up her sleeve. Leslie put the blood pressure cuff around her patient's arm before pulling the stethoscope from around her neck. As she was about to inflate the cuff, the examination door opened, an agency nurse named Linda peeked her head into the room after briefly knocking on the door.

"Excuse me Leslie, but you have a call holding on line 2," Linda said, smiling at the patient.

"Okay, thank you," Leslie replied. After completing Mrs. Davidson's vital signs and recording the data in her medical chart, Leslie walked to the nurse's station and picked up the phone, pushing the blinking light on the phone base.

"Leslie Johnson speaking, how may I help you?

"Hey, it's me Chris, I just wanted to call and see if we're still on for lunch today?" Leslie had forgotten all about having lunch with him today.

"Oh, ah sure, there's a small restaurant on the 1st floor called Buckley's. They serve pretty good lunch. I can't leave the building though because I have clinic this afternoon, and we have a lot of patients to see," Leslie said. She knew she should've told him no. Ed probably wouldn't have approved of her having lunch with the man they met at Tiger's last night. Since she didn't plan on doing anything sexual with him, she figured being friends wouldn't hurt anything. There was something about him that made her feel comfortable. "Okay, what time?" He asked.

"I should be finished with the morning clinic around 12:30pm. So, say 12:45, you know how to get here?" Leslie asked as she placed Mrs. Davidson's chart in the ben.

"Yep, see you in a few," Chris said before hanging up the phone. Chris smiled as he got out of the bed.

"Hey, it's time for you two to leave, I got somewhere to go." Chris said to the two women lying asleep in his bed. He walked over to his pants and pulled his wallet out of the back pocket. He pulled two $100 bills out and tossed them on the bed. The two young women grabbed the money and got dressed. After escorting the women out of his house and locking his front door, he walked back up the steps to the bathroom. He didn't want to be late for his lunch date. He began whistling as he turned on the shower.

It was around 1:15pm when Leslie finally entered the restaurant. She was hoping Chris hadn't arrived yet. No such luck, she spotted him sitting in the booth in the back.

“Sorry to keep you waiting, it’s been pretty busy today,” Leslie said as she slid into the booth.

“No problem at all,” he said smiling. They talked about simple things during lunch. They discussed everything from Chris’s real estate and entertainment business to the missionary trips Leslie took in college to help set up clinics in Africa. Before they knew it, half an hour had passed, and Leslie had to get back to work. Chris stood up and took her hand to help her out of the booth. Suddenly, Leslie blurted out,

“Do you have any plans for dinner tonight?”

“No,” Chris replied. Clearly surprised by her question.

“Ed is working late tonight, and I hate eating alone. Would you like to have dinner with me tonight?” She asked, biting her lower lip.

“I’d love to, just name the time and place.” He said grinning.

“7:00, at my place. Do you remember how to get there?” She asked.

“Yes, I’ll be there,” he said smiling.

“Great, see you then!” She said smiling as she walked away.

Leslie stepped into the elevator and pushed the number 7 button before stepping toward the back of the elevator. She leaned against the elevator wall as she thought about her lunch date with Chris. Leslie was tired of playing the fool. She was tired of being the good wife while her cheating husband continued to dishonor their wedding vows. She knew Ed didn't have a meeting scheduled at the office tonight. After years of dealing with his constant lies and cheating, Leslie had learned to double check anything Ed told her. When he walked out the door for work this morning, Leslie immediately called the law firm. She asked the receptionist if they were going to be open late tonight. The receptionist informed her that the building was scheduled to close early today due to some electrical maintenance issues. She said no one would be in the building after 3:00pm except for maintenance workers, but that the firm would reopen tomorrow at 9:00am. Normally, Leslie would have called Ed and went into a frenzy, but not this time. Leslie was getting tired of begging him to be faithful. She was tired of chasing after him. After getting off the phone this morning, Leslie sat down on the couch and cried. She knew her husband was back to his old ways. After seeing Chris today, Leslie decided it was time for her husband to get a taste of his own medicine. There was something about Chris that had her curious, and she was going to investigate. Leslie didn't know if she would actually sleep with him, but then she also wasn't going to promise that she wouldn't. When the elevator reached her floor, Leslie began humming a soft melody as she walked back toward the clinic.

Leslie's work day seemed to fly by. At 3:00pm she packed up her things and clocked out. Leslie normally traveled up Interstate 75N to go home. But today she decided to travel Interstate 285. "I can avoid traffic this way, "Leslie said out loud. Leslie turned up the volume on her car radio, listening to Alicia Keys sing "This Girl Is On Fire." For some reason Leslie felt happy, she couldn't wait to have dinner with Chris tonight.

Honk, Honk, Honk! Leslie realized an older lady in the left lane was blowing her horn and waving at her.

"Move your car over lady before you crash!" The woman yelled. Leslie was so deep in her thoughts that she hadn't realized that her lane was about to end due to construction. Leslie maneuvered her car into the empty space in front of the older woman's Buick Regal. She put her hand out the window and thanked the lady for the warning and for letting her over. Traffic was thick this afternoon. The only lane that was moving was the HOV lane. As Leslie sat in stand still traffic she decided to text Chris to let him know she might be a little late for dinner. As she began texting, she saw a flash out the corner of her eye. When she looked over, she saw a woman in a black Suburban SUV in the HOV lane taking pictures of her. The woman had a black scarf wrapped around her head, covering her face, leaving only her eyes and mouth visible. The lady snapped several more pictures of Leslie before speeding off. Leslie immediately jumped into the next opening in the HOV lane. She tried to follow the black Suburban, but it sped off getting too far out of Leslie's reach. Who was that lady and why was she taking pictures of me? "Leslie wondered.

An hour later, the black Suburban pulled up to a pool hall on Bankhead Highway. The woman whose identity was covered with the black scarf stepped out of the SUV and walked inside the smoke-filled pool hall carrying a briefcase. She walked over to a table occupied by three men.

Two of the men were large muscle-bound men sporting tattoo's all over their arms, necks, and face. They appeared to be gang affiliated. The other man was small in stature but well dressed. He was draped in jewelry and had gold rings on each finger. From his persona, it was obvious that he was the leader and not a man to be messed with. The woman sat down at the table and pulled a manila envelope out of her briefcase, sliding it toward the three men.

"Here are pictures of the woman, the man, and his wife." The lady said in a deep sultry voice. The leader picked up the envelope and pulled out several pictures of a woman, Ed, and Leslie. Some of the pictures were of the woman and Ed together, and some were pictures of Ed with Leslie, the rest were pictures of all of them separately.

"I just finished taking a few more pictures of the wife. I can have those developed and sent to you in a few days if you need close up pictures of her."

"Naw, this should be okay," he replied as he inspected all the pictures.

"My client said you'll get half now, and the other half once the job is complete," the woman said as she slid the briefcase across the table. The man opened the briefcase and pulled out a stack of hundred-dollar bills.

“Here’s $100,000 now and the remaining $100,000 once the job is complete.”

"Count it!" He ordered as he closed the briefcase and pushed it over to one of the other men sitting at the table. The large man picked up the briefcase and walked over to the bar. He pulled out a money counting machine from under the bar, sat it on the counter, and began running the bills through the machine. The woman sat in silence as the money was counted. Once the last bill was run through the machine, he turned toward the leader.

"$100,000," he announced as he put the money back into the briefcase and brought it back over to the table.

"Okay, so when does your boss want to get started?" The leader asked.

"As soon as possible. The instructions are in the envelope," she replied as she stood up from the table.

"Alright, give us a few days," he said as he lit a cigarette and took a long deep drag.

"Okay," she replied before walking out of the building and getting back into her SUV. She picked up her cell phone and called a number from her saved contacts. When the voice on the other end answered, she simply said. "It's done." Then she ended the call without waiting for a response. She pulled out of the parking lot and headed back toward the highway.

Chapter 4

At 7:30pm Mia pulled up to the restaurant. When she walked into the building, the host greeted her at the door.

"Table for two," Mia said. The host directed Mia to the back of the restaurant. As she followed the host she heard a voice. "Mia, Mia over here." It was Ed, he already had a table for them on the opposite side of the restaurant. Mia was intrigued by Ed's promptness. She thanked the host for his time and walked over to Ed.

"Hello Ed," Mia said, as she reached over and kissed him on the lips.

"Hi Sweetheart," Ed replied.

"Excuse me waiter," Ed called out, waving his arm at the male waiter. The waiter, a young college student, came over to the table.

"I would like to order my lovely date a Sex On The Beach and I'll have a couple of Coors."

Mia was ok with the drink Ed ordered for her. Sex On The Beach was her favorite drink. He must've remembered that from last night, Mia thought to herself. He was obviously a man who paid attention to his woman.

"I want to apologize about last night," Ed said once the waiter walked away.

"It's okay. I felt a special connection with you last night. Did you miss me?" Mia asked.

"Yes baby," Ed eagerly answered.

"What do you miss about me?"

"I miss the feeling of your soft lips on me," Ed answered truthfully.

"I miss tasting and pleasing you too baby," Mia seductively replied.

"What do you say to us finishing what we started last night?" Ed asked mischievously.

"I was just about to ask you the same question," Mia chuckled.

Dinner, three Sex on the Beaches, and six beers later, Mia and Ed decided to leave Smokey's. She followed Ed to a nearby motel. Mia waited in her car as Ed booked them a room. Once he had the keys, he walked over to the balcony.

"Room 122!" Ed yelled over the balcony to Mia. Mia grabbed her purse, turned off her cellphone, and got out of her car. She smiled as she locked the car doors. She took her time walking up the broken steps toward their room. This was not a four-star hotel, but it served the purpose, Mia thought to herself as she observed her surroundings.

"Baby what took you so long?" Ed chuckled. He was already in the bed completely undressed when she entered the room.

"I'm sorry honey," Mia laughed. "Wow he must really want me bad", she whispered to herself, "He didn't waste any time getting undressed," Mia chuckled. His manhood was so big and strong. Mia couldn't resist. She immediately undressed and joined Ed in bed. Mia slowly kissed Ed's dick.

"Is this what you've been waiting for?" Mia asked with in a naughty tone.

"Yes, Mia Yes," Ed moaned.

She began to move her mouth up and down his large shaft with slow, deliberate motions. Allowing her tongue to explore every crease and fold of his engorged manhood.

"Ahhh," ED moaned. Mia began focusing her attention to the shaft of his manhood, this drove Ed nuts. She licked, sucked, and twirled her tongue in a circular motion, all while she stared in Ed's eyes watching him helplessly lie in complete bliss.

"FUCK!" Ed screamed. Mia smiled as she slowed down her pace to keep him from busting an orgasm all over her. Mia began to lick his balls while giving him a hand job at the same time.

"Mia you're the best!" Ed screamed. She opened her mouth wide as she deep throated his manhood.

"OOOOOOOOOOOOOOOOOOOOHH HHHH MIAAAAAAAAA! Mia!" Ed yelled.

"Mia, Mia, Mia, Mia," Ed stuttered as an orgasm took over his body.

"Yes Ed," Mia replied smiling.

"You're freaking awesome! You belong to me now. I don't want you with no other man. Not even your husband!" Ed said aggressively as he lay on the bed. Mia laughed as she got out of the bed and walked over to the window. It had started raining. Mia watched as the rain drops began hitting the window.

“Chris isn’t really my husband. We just act like we’re married when we want to swing. I’m flattered that you want me all to yourself. Ed, I feel like maybe we’ve just experienced love at first sight. What do you think?” When there was no reply, Mia turned around and realized Ed was no longer in the room and hadn’t heard a thing she said.

"Ed, where are you?" Mia called out.

Ed put his hand over the cell phone speaker.

"I'm in the bathroom. Be out in a minute. You know I want a second round," Ed stated before putting his ear back to the phone. He had called Leslie's phone several times today but had been unsuccessful in reaching her. He dialed her number again but hung up as soon as the answering machine came on. He knew that Tuesday’s were a very busy day for her at the clinic and sometimes she had to stay over. She’s probably still at work, Ed thought to himself. He decided to call back and leave a message.

"Hey baby, just calling to check in. We still have a lot of things to go over at the office. I'm not sure what time we'll finish. We might go out for drinks afterward so don’t wait up. I should be home around midnight. I love you," he said into the phone before ending the call. He walked back into the room and back into Mia's waiting arms.

Chapter 5

When Leslie couldn't find the woman in the black SUV, she decided it was best that she head home. She ignored several calls from Ed today. She just couldn't deal with his lies anymore. She felt so overwhelmed, and her nerves were shot. She began to cry, and suddenly Chris was on her mind. She remembered how safe she had felt in his arms last night. She would give anything to feel that again. However, she contemplated canceling their dinner plans. She didn't want him to see her like this. All she wanted to do was take a hot bath and let the water soothe her, she thought as she drove through her neighborhood.

She was about to text Chris to cancel their date but stopped when she saw him sitting on her front steps waiting for her. She tried to hold her composure but as soon as he touched her, she began crying. She couldn't help it. She felt Chris wrap his arms around her and console her until the tears subsided. She wiped her eyes and unlocked the front door. Once they entered the house, and without saying a word, Chris picked her up and carried her up the steps to her bathroom. She felt like he must have been reading her mind because he placed her on the toilet and began running bathwater for her. He helped her undress, still not saying anything. Next, he helped her step into the tub.

"All I want you to do is relax. I'll order us something to eat," he said as he began to walk away. Leslie grabbed his arm before he could leave.

"Please don't leave me," she pleaded. Chris couldn't refuse her. He began taking off his clothes and jewelry. Leslie couldn't help but admire his body. He was a handsome man. He was fit, strong, and, just beautiful, she thought. Leslie was lost in her thoughts and didn't realize Chris was watching her stare at him. He began to laugh.

"Enjoying the view?" He asked.

"Very much, thank you!" She replied. Chris laughed again and slid into the tub behind her, wrapping his arms around her waist. Leslie sighed, she wished she could stay like this forever.

"What're you thinking about?" Chris asked as he picked up a washcloth and began to splash warm water on her breast.

"Thinking that I can't believe I'm actually cheating on my husband. In 8 years, no matter how many times I found out he cheated on me, I was never unfaithful. I've known my husband ever since I was thirteen. He's the first and only man I've ever been with," she whispered.

"What made you choose me?" He asked as he placed the washcloth back in the water and brought up new bubbled bath water to splash across her chest.

"I'm tired of being hurt. I guess there's something about you that makes me feel like you can help my pain go away, even if it's only temporary," she replied. She sat up in the tub and turned around to face him. She got on her knees and moved in between his legs. She lowered her head and began kissing his lips. Chris enjoyed the feel of her soft lips and the sweet taste of her tongue. After a long passionate kiss, Chris got out of the tub and held out his hand to help her out. Leslie knew what was on his mind. His large thick manhood was standing at attention. She took his hand and allowed him to help her out of the tub.

"We can't do anything in my bedroom, we'll have to go to the guest room," Leslie whispered as she allowed Chris to dry her body with a towel.

"I understand, you want to go to the room we were in last night?" He asked as he bent down and rubbed the soft towel over her legs.

"Yes," she whispered. Chris took the towel and quickly dried himself before turning around and lifting Leslie in his arms and carrying her down the steps toward the guest room. Leslie felt so happy and unsure at the same time. Once they reached the guest room, Chris gently placed Leslie back on her feet. As much as she wanted to do to Ed what he had done to her so many times, she just couldn't do it.

"I'm sorry Chris, but I can't do this," Leslie said as she stared into Chris's eyes. She could tell he was disappointed and frustrated, but he held his composure well.

"I understand," Chris replied before walking out the room. They both got dressed and then went back to the living room.

"Wow, I see you have Scrabble, my favorite board game. Let me beat you real quick. I'm the best at this game," Chris stated arrogantly as he rubbed both his hands together with a smirk on his face.

"Fine, I hope you're as good as you say you are because I've never lost a game once!" Leslie said with a huge smile. They were interrupted when her cell phone began ringing. She walked over to the table and picked it up as Chris set up the game. She saw her husband's name and phone number flash across the screen. She pushed the ignore button on her phone. Ed called right back and left a message. Leslie waited briefly before dialing her voicemail and listening to the message. She sighed as she listened to Ed lie about the meeting and going out with friends for drinks after work. After listening to his message, she dialed a local Chinese restaurant that delivered and ordered food for her and Chris. Then placed her phone on vibrate before walking back over to the table. Leslie had the time of her life. Scrabble had always been her favorite game.

"I'm the winner!" Leslie yelled proudly.

"I let you win. You're so beautiful, I couldn't see you as anything but a winner." Chris said as he leaned over and kissed Leslie on her lips. Leslie realized she hadn't laughed so hard or been so happy in quite a while.

After dinner and another game of Scrabble, Leslie glanced at the clock on the wall.

"It's getting late. You should leave before Ed comes home," Leslie said as she began cleaning up.

"I enjoyed every moment with you tonight. When will we see each other again?" Chris asked.

"I'm not sure, I'll call you. Do you mind taking the trash out when you go?" She asked. She didn't want Ed to find the two Chinese dinner containers.

"Sure, no problem," Chris said as he picked up the bag of trash.

"I enjoyed spending time with you tonight, and I promise I'll call," Leslie said as she glanced at her watch. It was getting late, she knew Ed would be home at any minute.

"Okay love, I'll be waiting for your call," Chris said as he kissed Leslie before walking out the front door. Leslie watched as Chris got in his car and drove away. Thirty minutes later Ed pulled into the driveway.

"Hello Sweetheart, I thought you would be sleep by now. I called you several few times today," Ed said as he walked into the bedroom.

"Yea, I'm still awake. I thought I would finish the rest of this book before I went to sleep. How was your meeting?" Leslie asked as she turned a page of her book.

"Oh, the same as usual, nothing spectacular. We're trying to get ready for trial," Ed replied as he kissed Leslie on the forehead.

"Are you hungry?" Leslie asked.

"No, we grabbed something after the meeting. I'm just tired. All I want to do is take a shower and go to sleep," Ed said as he began to undress. As he walked into the bathroom, he noticed a man's watch along with a business card sitting on the sink.

"What the Hell?" Ed said as he picked up the watch and business card. After reading the card, he placed the card and the watch back on the bathroom sink. After taking his shower, he picked up the watch and card and headed for his bedroom. When Ed walked back into the bedroom, Leslie was sitting up against pillows in the bed still reading.

"How was work today?" Ed asked as he sat down on the bed.

"It was alright." She replied. Ed stared at her for a while before speaking again.

"I found this in our bathroom this evening," he said as he laid the watch and business card in front of her on the bed. Leslie looked at Chris's belongings and felt her heart drop. She did her best to keep a straight face.

"I think it belongs to the guy that was here last night. Wasn't his name Chris or something like that? He must have left it last night," Leslie said as she picked up the business card and read it.

"I don't remember seeing it when I took a shower this morning." Ed said frowning.

"I don't remember seeing it either. We must have overlooked it," she said nonchalantly.

"Well, I'll return them to him tomorrow," Ed said as he picked up the watch and business card and placed them back on the stand. He began putting his things away, turned off the lamp, and laid down on his side facing the window. Leslie followed him, also turning on her side in the opposite direction. Neither one bothered to touch the other.

Leslie woke up the next morning to see the sun peeking through her window blinds. She turned over and looked at her husband before sitting up straight and throwing her legs over the side of the bed. She walked over to the window, pulling back the curtains to allow the morning sun to enter the room. She glanced at Chris's watch and business card on the nightstand. Should I grab it, and take it to Chris myself? Leslie asked herself. No, it's no big deal. Ed will return it to him and all will be fine. Leslie thought to herself as she walked out of the bedroom, and down the steps toward the kitchen to make some fresh coffee." Thirty minutes later Ed walked into the kitchen fully dressed.

"Good morning honey," Leslie said with a bright smile.

"Morning Leslie" Ed replied in a very dry tone.

"Coffee?" Leslie asked.

"No thank you," Ed said as he walked towards the counter. He pulled a white envelope out of one of the kitchen drawers, putting the watch and business card inside before walking toward the front door.

"I'm off to work; I'll be home early for dinner!" Ed barked. He obviously isn't in a good mood this morning, Leslie thought to herself. She knew it probably had something to do with finding Chris's things in the bathroom.

"Okay honey," Leslie said sweetly as Ed left the kitchen.

Ed normally went straight to his office when he arrived at work, but this morning, he stopped by his assistant's desk first.

"Lucille, I need for you to come by my office as soon as you get a second."

"Yes sir," she replied. She immediately ended her call and followed Ed down the hall to his office.

"Good morning Ed, what do you need?"

"I need for you to send this watch and business card to the address and name on the card," Ed ordered.

"I'm right on it Sir," Lucille said as she grabbed the watch and card.

"Oh yea, add a little note that says. Stay the Fuck away from my wife!!!!" Ed yelled with pure rage in his eyes while banging his fist on the office desk.

"Yes sir," Lucille said nervously as she left his office. As she walked down the hallway, the entire office staff was staring and whispering.

"Is everything ok?" Asked a fellow employee.

"Yes, everything's fine," Lucille quickly replied. Lucille went to her desk, prepared the letter, went to the mail room, and had the letter delivered. She wondered what was going on with Ed and his wife. She thought Leslie was such a nice and gentle woman. Ed's numerous extra-marital affairs were no secret at the law firm. As she returned to her desk, a young woman stepped off the elevator and walked to her desk.

"Hello, my name is Tammy Morrison, I have an appointment to see Edward Johnson Jr," she said smiling. After finding her name in her appointment book, Lucille escorted Tammy Morrison into Ed's office.

"Hello Ed."

"Hello Tammy, what can I do for you?"

"Is that the way you greet all your ex-lovers?" Tammy asked as she sat down in the chair in front of his desk.

"Sorry, what's up?" Ed asked impatiently. He hated when the women wouldn't let go once he decided the affair was over.

"Why have you been avoiding me?" She demanded.

"I haven't been avoiding you. I've just been busy that's all," he shrugged as he shuffled through the paperwork on his desk.

"I heard about Sandy trying to run your wife down with her car. She should've run you over instead."

"Okay, I'm sure you didn't come all the way down here to discuss Sandy and my wife. What do you want Tammy? I'm really busy."

"I've been calling and leaving you messages on your phone for the last two months. You've never returned any of my calls. Is that how you treat all the women you fuck over? Once you see a new piece of pussy, you just drop the old one like a bad habit? You were seeing Sandy at the same time you were seeing me! The least you could've done was mess with someone I didn't know. You're such an asshole!"

"Tammy!" Ed warned.

"I don't know why your wife stays with you. You're a fucking jerk. One day you're going to fuck with the wrong woman!" Tammy yelled.

"Tammy, you've already received your check from the firm this month. I hope you didn't come down here trying to get more money. Because if you did, I can tell your right now the answer is NO! You won't get more than we agreed upon. So, I advise you to get your ass out of my office!" He yelled pointing toward the door.

"I'm pregnant and you're the father, you Son of a Bitch!" Tammy screamed. Ed suddenly turned colors.

"Pregnant? What the fuck are you talking about? We only fucked a few times, and I wore protection!"

"Yes, but don't you remember the night the condom broke? That must have been the night I got pregnant because I haven't slept with anyone else since that night. You're the only man I've been with in over six months," Tammy said standing up and putting her hands on his desk.

"Okay so what? Did you come for more money to pay for an abortion? How much do you need?" Ed asked as he pulled out his check book and picked up a pen.

"Abortion? I'm not having an abortion. I'm keeping our baby."

"What the fuck do you mean you're keeping it?" He yelled. He lowered his voice after realizing that someone outside the office may have heard him.

"You know you can't keep it, I'm a married man!" He whispered with anger.

"You didn't care about being married when you were fucking me now did you? I'm keeping this baby. I came down here to tell you that you need to inform your precious little wife that I'm about to have your first child in six months." Tammy yelled before walking out the office slamming the door behind her. She walked briskly down the aisle towards the elevators. She acted as if she didn't see the shocked faces of the office staff staring at her as she stepped into the elevator.

Ed's face was drained of color. If Leslie found out he had fathered a child outside their marriage it would hurt her deeply. One of Leslie's greatest desires was to become a mother. They had been trying to have children for the last eight years. But after four miscarriages, the doctor told Leslie her womb might not be strong enough to bear children. Ed had tried to talk to her about adopting, but she was so devastated she wouldn't even discuss it. Ed knew that getting another woman pregnant was something Leslie would never forgive.

"Oh my God what have I done? I'm about to lose my wife!" Ed yelled as he put his head into his hands and began sobbing.

Chapter 6

Driving down the busy streets of Atlanta, Mia sped her way through traffic to get to Chris's office. She quickly parked her car in the garage and ran into the office building. Mia walked into his office and handed him an envelope with money and sales receipts, as she was walking out the office Chris's cell phone rang.

"Hello" Chris answered. It was Leslie.

"Hello Chris, how are you?"

"I'm fine Beautiful, what's on your mind today?"

"'I'm calling because Ed found your watch and business card on the bathroom floor and said he was going to return it to you. Have you heard from him?"

"No, I haven't heard from him. I knew I left that watch somewhere. I've been looking all over for it. I'll call you when I receive it."

"Ok. Thanks! Have a good day."

"Wait" Chris yelled before Leslie had a chance to end the call. I did receive a package earlier maybe this is it. Let me open it, hold on." Chris said as he laid the phone down and opened the small package. He pulled out his watch, his business card, and a letter. He began to read the message. "Stay the Fuck away from my wife!" Chris smiled vindictively.

"Leslie are you still there?" He asked after picking up the phone back up.

"Yes, I'm still here. Was the package from Ed?"

"Yes, and I think he knows I was at your house," Chris stated.

"What makes you say that?" Leslie asked nervously.

"Because he sent me a personal note and told me to stay away from you." He chuckled.

"No, I don't think he knows, he's probably just threatening you. Listen I have to go, I'll talk to you later." Leslie stated and abruptly hung up the phone. Chris leaned back in his chair and laughed as he read the note again.

Leslie left work earlier than normal. On her way home, she decided to stop at the supermarket to pick up items for Ed's favorite meal. Steak, potatoes, and salad. Ed loved Leslie's cooking. She figured a good home cooked meal and a heated lovemaking session, would help ease some of the tension between them.

While in the frozen food section she ran into her old friend Gloria. They'd been friends since middle school. It was Gloria who first introduced her to Ed. Ed couldn't stand Gloria because he said she always meddled in their relationship. Gloria couldn't stand Ed either. She used to beg Leslie to leave Ed, telling her that she deserved better. Before she got married, Gloria and Leslie had a bad argument about her relationship with Ed. Leslie had felt offended and disrespected. Although they eventually made up, their friendship was never the same after that. Leslie hadn't spoken to Gloria in almost a year. She decided that if she was going to work on rebuilding her marriage, she needed to stay away from any negative outside influences.

"Hey lady, long time no hear. How've you been? You look beautiful as usual." Gloria said smiling.

"I'm fine, I've been working a lot of hours at the clinic and working on rebuilding my marriage," Leslie said proudly as she picked up frozen carrots and threw them into her grocery cart.

"I'm glad you and Ed were able to work through things. When I heard about that girl getting pregnant, I just knew it was finally over between you two. But I'm glad you were able to work through it." Leslie's mouth dropped open.

"What're you talking about Gloria? What pregnant girl?" Leslie asked frowning. Gloria shook her head, realizing that once again she was the bearer of bad news about Ed. She wouldn't have said anything if she had known that Leslie didn't know. Gloria knew how badly Leslie wanted children.

"Ahh, I thought you knew. I'm so sorry Leslie." Gloria whispered.

"What girl is pregnant Gloria?" Leslie repeated.

"Leslie, I don't want to be spreading any rumors. Maybe you should talk to the young lady yourself. Her name is Tammy Morrison. She's one of my coworkers. I'll give you her phone number." Gloria said as she pulled out her cellphone, a piece of paper, and a pen from her purse. After finding Tammy's number in her call log, she wrote it down and handed it to Leslie.

"Thanks," Leslie said as she snatched the paper and walked out the store without bothering to say goodbye to Gloria or purchase anything.

Leslie walked out to her car and sat down in the driver's seat. She pulled out the piece of paper Gloria had given her. Should she call? What if it was just a rumor? What if Gloria had lied? She wanted to believe that so bad, but in all the years Leslie had known Gloria, she had never lied to her. Leslie knew she wasn't going to be able to relax until she talked to this woman. She pulled out her cell phone and dialed the number. She could feel her palms starting to sweat as she waited for Tammy to answer the phone.

"Hello," Tammy answered.

"Hello, is ah, is this um Tammy Morrison?" Leslie asked as her voice trembled.

"Yes, who is this?" Tammy asked. Tammy already knew it was Ed's wife. She had heard

Leslie’s voice many times on the answering machine when Ed would take her to his house for a quickie.

"This is Leslie Johnson, Edward Johnson Jr.’s wife. I have something I would like to ask you," Leslie said slowly.

“Okay, what is it?”

“Um”, Leslie paused. “I just ran into an old friend who said you were pregnant by my ah husband, is this ah true?” Leslie stuttered.

“Mrs. Johnson, I don't...um... know how to say this gently, so I'm just going to say it. Yes, I am pregnant by Ed. Ed and I have been having an affair on and off for about two years.”

“Are you sure Ed is the father?” Leslie asked as she felt her throat begin to tighten.

"Yes, I’m positive. I don’t have a problem having a paternity test done as soon as the baby’s born if you need proof," Tammy replied confidently.

“You’re keeping the baby?” Leslie whispered?

“Oh yes, I love this baby already,” Tammy replied proudly. Unable to control herself, Leslie ended the call, before dropping the phone and bursting into tears. Leslie sat in the parking lot for what seemed like hours, crying uncontrollably. She continued to cry all the way home. "Why! Why would you do this to me Ed? How could you betray me like this!" Leslie screamed as she banged her fist against the steering wheel.

When she finally reached her house, she felt so weak that she could barely get out of the car. When she walked into her house, she became filled with rage. She began smashing dishes, breaking lamps, pulling things out of drawers and smashing framed pictures. When she finally managed to calm down, she picked up a piece of paper and pen off the floor. She was crying as she began writing her husband a letter.

"I gave you my entire young life. I worshipped the ground you walked on because I loved you so much. I tried to be understanding. I tried to overlook all the times you betrayed me. I tried going to counseling. I tried everything I could to save our marriage! I can't do this anymore. Today I found out that you've gotten one of your Bitches pregnant. How could you betray me like this? How could you hurt me like this! Don't worry you bastard, you've hurt me for

the last time! I'm leaving you Ed! I want a divorce! It's over between us!!!!!!"

After writing the letter, Leslie ran upstairs and pulled out two suitcases. She packed as much as she could fit into the two suitcases. She continued to cry as she left the note on the bed before walking out the door. As she got into her car, she pulled out her cell phone and called her lawyer.

"I need a meeting with you as soon as possible. I want to file for a divorce."

Chapter 7

Ed locked his office door, got in his vehicle and traveled home. The ride home was long as usual. When he walked into his house, he was shocked at the condition of the house. His first thought was that someone had broken in.

“Leslie! He screamed as he ran up the steps to their bedroom. He immediately noticed the letter on the bed. He was almost afraid to read it. But relaxed slightly when he realized it was Leslie’s handwriting. But that relaxed feeling didn’t last long as he read the letter. He grabbed the phone and dialed her number. The voice mail came on almost immediately. He kept calling and leaving messages for her to call him. But she never picked up the phone or called him back. Ed dropped to his knees and began to cry out.

"Leslie where are you!!! What have I done?” He sobbed. He grabbed his keys and ran out the house looking for her, he drove up and down the street for hours. He stopped by all her friends and family member's homes, hoping she was at someone's house but had no luck with finding her. He finally gave up and went home. He picked up the phone and called one of his friends.

"Hey it's me Ed. I have a major problem. I need your help!"

"No problem, I have a pretty busy schedule, but I can meet you tomorrow night," his friend replied as he cleared his deep voice.

"Okay I'll meet you at the diner," Ed said before ending the call. Ed was so distraught he began to think of Mia, he needed sex, it was the only way he could cope with stress. He knew he shouldn't, but his hormones were raging out of control. He phoned Mia and asked her to meet him immediately, and she agreed.

They met at the same hotel. Mia was dressed in a red sexy dress and smelled so good. She began undressing Ed as soon as they walked through the door. She put her fingers over his mouth, indirectly asking him not to speak. She wrapped her soft lips around his manhood, she already knew what he wanted. Ed felt his legs grow weak. Mia licked the shaft of his manhood, then proceeded to wrap her lips around the head. She focused her attention there for a while. Ed squirmed and moaned loudly. Mia stared into Ed's eyes as she went up and down slowly, up and down, up and down. She could feel Ed's dick growing larger and this turned her on. "Fuck my throat Ed Johnson," Mia moaned. Ed jumped up, flipped Mia around, put on a condom, and began pounding away at her womanhood. Mia screamed in both pleasure and pain as Ed continued to give her womanhood a serious beat down. Mia handled him like a professional. Ed thrust faster moaning and screaming with every thrust.

"Fill me up with your juices Ed," Mia screamed. Ed lost control.

"LESLIEEEEEEEEEEEEEEEE!!!!!!" Ed screamed as his body shook from the power of the orgasm.

Mia was pissed! Had he just yelled out his wife's name during sex? Disgusted, she quickly cleaned up and left without saying a word. As soon as Mia walked out the door, Ed reached for his cell phone and dialed Leslie's number over and over again. She was still ignoring his calls. He finally dropped the cell phone on the floor and began sobbing like a baby.

Leslie continued to ignore Ed’s calls. She called her job and informed her supervisor that she was taking a leave of absence due to a family emergency. After her supervisor had hung up, Leslie dialed Chris's number.

"Hello."

"Hey Chris, it's me Leslie."

"What's wrong baby? I can tell from the tone of your voice that something's not right."

"I left Ed."

"You left Ed?" Chris immediately stood up and began pacing the floor.

"Yes, I'm filing for a divorce. It's over between us, I'm through."

"Where are you?”

"I'm at a resort in Columbus, Georgia."

"How long will you be staying there?”

“I don’t know. Maybe a few weeks.”

“Text me the name and the address, I'm coming to see you this weekend," Chris said before ending the call. He picked up the cellphone and dialed Mia.

"Hello?"

"Hey there's going to be a small change to the plan, I'll tell you the details later," Chris said before ending the call. He sat back down in his chair in disbelief and happiness all at the same time. Chris looked at his phone and saw the text from Leslie with the address of the hotel. He smiled as he put the phone down on his desk and began going through files on his desk.

Ed walked into the Waffles & Wine on Old National Highway. He looked around the cafe until he spotted his longtime friend Jason sitting in a booth next to a window in the back of the restaurant. Jason had a receding hairline, a big beer belly, and a laugh that reminded him of Santa Claus.

"Hey Jason, thanks for meeting me."

"No problem man," Jason said standing up. They gave each other a brotherly pat on the back before sitting down.

"Man, you look like you haven't slept in days. What's going on?" Before Ed had a chance to answer, a young, pretty waitress walked up to the table.

"Hey Ed, hey Jason, do you two want your usual or do you want to try something new?" She asked.

"I thought you only worked on Tuesday and Thursday afternoons, what're you doing here so late?" Jason asked.

"I'm covering for Cindy tonight. Her son's sick."

"Oh, okay. Is it just me or do you look sexier and sexier every time I see you?" Jason asked flirting.

"You so crazy," Carmen said laughing. Ed and Jason had been meeting at Waffles & Wine for years. Whenever the waitresses saw them enter the restaurant, they would start arguing to see who would get their section. Ed and Jason always left fifty-dollar tips.

"Yes, I'll have my regular," Ed interrupted in a dry voice. Ed would normally have joined in with flirting with Carmen. But today he was in no flirting mood.

"Yea I'll have my regular too. Hey Carmen, if you ever decide to leave that broke boyfriend of yours, I'll be waiting. You need to give me a chance. I'll treat you like a beautiful queen should be treated," Jason said smiling.

"Okay, I'll keep that in mind. Just don't forget my tip," Carmen laughed as she walked away switching her hips.

"Man, if I were ten years younger I'd take Carmen from her boyfriend," Jason said laughing as he watched Carmen walk away.

"If you were ten years younger you would still be partially bald, fat, and married to Samantha," Ed chuckled. Jason had a way of getting Ed out of even the darkest moods. They'd been friends since high school. It was Ed who introduced Jason to Samantha when they were in high school. Jason had joined the Marines straight out of high school, and Ed had gone on to college, but they never lost contact with each other.

"Whatever, you know I'm never going to marry that woman. She's crazy as hell!" Jason laughed. "Okay man, so tell me what's going on?" Jason asked, his facial expression quickly turning serious.

"Leslie left me."

"Leslie left? Really when?" Jason asked.

"Yesterday. A tramp I use to mess with told her that I got her pregnant," Ed mumbled.

"Is she really pregnant? Is the baby yours?"

"I don't know. If she is, it could be mine. I mean I did sleep with her. I guess it's a possibility." Ed shrugged his shoulders as he looked out the window.

"Man, I'm sorry to hear that. I know I shouldn't be saying this to you right now, but how long did you think you were going to be able to keep cheating on Leslie? I've been warning you for years to chill out, especially after that crazy girl tried to run her over."

"I know," Ed whispered.

"So, what's the favor you need from me?"

"I need you to find Leslie. She disappeared, and I need to find her. I want to make things right between us. I love my wife Jason, and I don't want to lose her. I know I'm not perfect, and I've done a lot to hurt her. But she's my oxygen. I can't lose her. I love her Jason," Ed sobbed.

Ed’s law firm had been using Jason's investigation company for many years. Jason was always able to find a missing person, have a person followed, or find important evidence needed to defend Ed's clients. Ed's father had been so impressed with Jason's company that he hired Jason for all the law firm’s investigation needs.

“No problem, I'll get right on it."

"I also want you to check out another person for me," Ed said as he passed Jason a large folder. Jason pulled out several pictures of Chris along with a sheet of paper with Chris’s name and business address on it.

"Who’s Chris Peterson?" Jason asked with raised eyebrows as he read the paper and looked at the photos.

"Someone I want you to keep an eye on," Ed replied.

Carmen walked over to the table carrying a tray. She placed their food in front of them. Jason winked at Carmen, and she began giggling before walking away from the table. The two men continued to talk late into the night.

Chapter 8

As Chris traveled down the highway headed toward Columbus, Georgia, he turned up the radio. The relaxing sound of jazz filled the car. The traffic was jammed for miles ahead. As he waited for traffic to begin moving again, Chris pulled out his cell phone and made a call to Leslie, he frowned when the answering machine came on. He decided to leave a message.

"Hey baby, I'm on my way. I'm stuck in a traffic, but I'll be there soon." Chris said before ending the call. Once the traffic started moving, Chris realized there had been an accident. After finally getting passed the accident, he got off at the next exit and drove to a gas station. Chris didn't notice the blue car behind him. He pumped his gas and then got back on the highway and continued his travel. He was so consumed with his thoughts that he never noticed the blue Dodge was still following him.

After finally reaching the luxurious 5-star hotel, Chris gave his keys to the valet before taking the elevator up to the 30th floor.

"Room 3011, there you are," Chris said. When he knocked on the door, Leslie swung the door open and practically jumped into his arms, almost knocking him to the floor. She kissed and hugged him as if she hadn't seen him in years.

"What a welcome," Chris chuckled as he picked her up and carried her into the room, kicking the door closed with his foot and walking over to the bed.

"Okay let's talk about what happened. Why did you leave Ed?"

"He got another woman pregnant, and I can't accept that. I'm so tired of the lies and disrespect Chris. I'm tired of the cheating. I'm done with that marriage!"

"I just don't understand why he couldn't appreciate a woman as beautiful as you. If you were my wife, I'd treat you like the queen you are," Chris said as he grabbed Leslie's face and kissed her.

"Make love to me Chris," Leslie softly said as she stared into Chris's eyes.

"Are you sure?"

"Yes, I'm sure." Chris laid Leslie across the bed.

"You're so beautiful." He said as he gazed into her eyes. Chris had been fantasizing about this moment ever since their first kiss.

"Thank you, baby," Leslie said as she ran the palm of her hand gently across his cheek. Chris took her hand and kissed it before lowering his head. He began to kiss her. His lips held her lower lip hostage sucking on it before allowing his tongue to take a journey into her warm moist mouth. Their tongues began dancing to their own tune. For a moment, time seemed to stand still as they explored the taste and touch of each other's lips. Chris helped Leslie remove her blouse. He felt his manhood stand at attention as the smell of her sweet perfume filled his nostrils. He inhaled deeply as he helped her remove her breast from their cotton prison. He lowered his head and began to suck on her breast. He took his time exploring each nipple. He loved her big breast. He had always been a breast and ass man.

"That feels so good baby," Leslie moaned. She was determined to block out any images of Ed from her mind and enjoy making love to another man. In her mind, her marriage was over. Chris was so handsome, and he made her feel special. Chris stood up and pulled off his pants and pulled out a Trojan from his pocket. Leslie took off her pants and thongs as she watched him roll the condom on his rock-hard penis. He reached for Leslie and turned her around, bending her over, and entering her womanhood from the back. He allowed his penis to feel the depths of her warmth. He couldn't resist. He began moving his hips back and forth quickly. He felt spasms run through his legs as he savored in the sensation.

"Baby you don't have to rush," Leslie said softly. She was slightly annoyed that Chris wasn't taking more time with foreplay instead of rushing straight to intercourse. Leslie gripped the edge of the bed to keep herself from falling as Chris rocked her body back and forth.

"Oh, ohh, yes. I know baby, but it's so good," he mumbled. Suddenly his body went tense.

"Ah, yes, baby, oh my you have some good pussy!" Chris yelled out in passion. After releasing his orgasmic juices, Chris fell onto the bed and began removing the condom. For a moment Leslie didn't move, she couldn't move. Had this man just fucked her for a total of 3 minutes? Ed always made sure she was fully aroused, and he never allow himself to have an orgasm until she had one first. Was Chris serious? Is this how sex with him would be? Maybe he was the type that liked to do it multiple times, and that was just a quick warm up, she thought to herself as she stared at him.

"Yes, baby that was good," Leslie smiled as she got back in bed and straddled his legs, she took his limp manhood in her hand and began to massage it, but Chris immediately pushed her hand away.

"No baby, don't touch him right now, he's too sensitive," Chris said as he crossed his forearm over his eyes. Leslie couldn't believe it.

"Come and lay next to me baby," Chris said as he patted the empty space next to him with his hand. Leslie laid down next to him and began staring at the television. Damn, all the frustration that was built up from Ed, and this is what I get? Three minutes of fame? Chris had some making up to do," Leslie thought to herself. Leslie heard her cell phone vibrating in her purse. "It's probably Ed blowing up my phone. After that lame sexual encounter I just had with Chris, I wish Ed were here to make my toes curl," Leslie mumbled to herself.

"What did you say baby?" Chris asked smiling as he turned over to look at her.

"Oh nothing, I was just saying I need to see who keeps blowing up my phone," she replied as she got up from the bed and grabbed her purse. She pulled out her phone, and she scrolled through the phone log. She wasn't surprised to see twenty missed calls from Ed. She put the phone back in her purse and walked into the bathroom. After cleaning herself, she walked back into the bed room. Chris was standing in front of the mirror naked as a Jaybird and smiling.

"Am I the best lover or what?" Chris asked as he did a silly dance in front of the mirror.

"Why didn't he have this much energy during sex?" Leslie mumbled to herself.

"What did you say baby?" He asked as he turned around.

"Oh, nothing," Leslie responded in a dry tone.

"What's wrong baby? Do you regret making love to me? Do you feel it was too soon?" Chris asked with a worried look on his face. Immediately Leslie felt bad. Chris was such a sweet man. She thought to herself as she walked over to him.

"No Chris, I don't regret a thing, I'm happy we had the opportunity to grow closer," Leslie replied as she grabbed Chris's hand and led him back to the bed. Chris's manhood immediately stood at attention. He reached for another condom on the nightstand and rolled it on. He grabbed Leslie's breasts and sucked on them for a few minutes before positioning Leslie so that he could enter her from behind. One stroke, "Ahh", two strokes, "Ahh," three strokes, "Ahhhh," Chris released himself again. Is this a freaking joke? Leslie thought. He rolled over and this time he fell asleep.

"I see I have a lot of work to do with this man, but he's worth the effort," Leslie whispered to herself as she laid her head on his chest.

The next morning Leslie woke up to the sun beaming on her face. She jumped in the shower and hummed her favorite melodies as beads of hot water beat against her back. The steam from the hot water filled the bathroom. Leslie reached for her Silver Bullet and began to massage her clit. Leslie had gotten quite familiar with her vibrator over the course of her marriage. Ed loved to watch her masturbate before making love to her. After climaxing, Leslie jumped out of the shower and got dressed. As she walked out of the bathroom, she overheard Chris on the phone. Leslie paused behind the door to listen.

"No, I already told you, just wait, we don't need to act yet. I'll let you know when," Chris said as he hung up the phone. Leslie entered the room.

"Good morning Sweetheart. Who was that?"

"Oh Mia, just talking business. Did you sleep well last night?" He asked.

"Yes, I slept like a baby. Would you like breakfast?" Leslie asked smiling. She relaxed when she realized it was Mia he was talking too. She didn't want to have to compete with another woman for his affection.

"Breakfast sounds good," Chris replied.

"You're going to need your energy for what I have in mind after we eat," Leslie said with excitement in her voice.

"What's going through that pretty little head of yours?" Chris asked.

"You'll find out after we eat," Leslie giggled, blushing as she walked over to the phone and ordered room service.

Chapter 9

Ed finished the last of his beer before crushing the can in his hand and tossing it with the other eight crushed beer cans in the middle of the living room floor. Ed had been drinking all night. He kept checking his cell phone to see if he had any missed calls from Leslie or Jason. Where could she have gone? He felt miserable without her. He hadn't slept in their bed since the day she left. She'd only been gone for about a week, but it felt like a life-time. He stopped by Tammy's house on the way home from work today. He wanted to try to reason with her, hoping to talk her into having the abortion. But she let him know that there was no way she was going to terminate her pregnancy. He left Tammy's house feeling hopeless and defeated. Ed picked up the remote control and turned on the television, the show Cheaters came on. He was in no mood to be reminded of what he had done. As he was flicking the remote control from one channel to the next his phone rang. He fumbled as he picked up the cell phone.

"Hello?" Ed slurred.

"Hey man, it's me Jason. I found her. She has a suite at the Hilton Estate Resort in Columbus, Georgia, and she isn't alone," Jason stated. Ed sat straight up on the couch.

"What do you mean she's not alone? Who's there with her?"

"I followed that guy Chris there. It looks like he may have spent the night with her. I waited until about 11:00 this morning, but he never came out." Rage began to build within Ed.

"What the fuck is he doing there with my wife? What room is she in? I'm driving down there right now!" Ed yelled with slurred speech as he stood up from the couch and began pacing the floor.

"I don't advise going down there right now, it's late and you sound like you're intoxicated. Wait until tomorrow, and I'll go with you." Jason replied.

"I don't need you to go with me. What's her room number?"

"They wouldn't give me her room number, but I do have the resort phone number, why don't you just call her."

"Okay, what's the number?" Ed asked as he began searching for a pen and paper.

“The number is 706-222-3333. When you call, just ask for her and they’ll ring her room. If you decide to drive down there, I'm going with you," Jason said sternly.

"Okay man, I'll call you back after I talk to her," Ed said before ending the call. He immediately dialed the resort. Just as Jason had said, the front desk clerk refused to release Leslie's room number but agreed to forward the call to her room. Ed waited patiently as the phone rang. His heart dropped when Chris picked up the phone.

"Hello," Chris answered.

"What the fuck are you doing with my wife! Where’s Leslie!" Ed screamed into the phone.

"I'm sorry sir, but you must have the wrong room. I don't know anyone named Charlie," Chris promptly hung up the phone and disconnected the line without Leslie knowing. When Leslie came back in the room, she asked, "Who was on the phone?"

"Wrong number," Chris replied nonchalantly.

"I know it's dinner time, but I have a taste for some more breakfast food. So, what'll it be pancakes or French toast, bacon or sausage links? Oh, and how would you like your eggs?" Leslie asked as she looked through the menu.

"French toast, sausage, & scrambled eggs sound wonderful babe."

As Leslie headed towards the hotel phone, Chris walked into the bathroom and called Mia back.

"We have a problem."

Ed sat there shocked for a moment until he realized what had just happened.

"That bastard!" He screamed. Ed immediately tried to call Leslie's room at least three more times but couldn't get through.

"I'm sorry sir, but the room you're trying to reach is unavailable. Would you like to leave a message?" The hotel clerk asked. Drunk and furious Ed slammed the phone down and called Jason.

"Jason, this is the last straw!" Ed slurred; I'm going down there to confront him NOW!" Ed screamed into the phone.

"Hold on man. I'm on my way to get you. There's no sense in doing anything stupid." Jason said hoping to calm Ed down.

“The bastard is in a hotel room with my wife! What do you expect me to do just sit here?” Ed screamed.

“Listen, I know you’re upset, but going over there now while you’re intoxicated is not the answer. You want to land yourself in jail?” Ed was quiet as he thought about what Jason said.

“Listen, I’m on my way over to your house.”

“Okay! But hurry up!” Ed said before hanging up.

Ed was pacing the floor when Jason finally whipped his blue dodge into Ed’s driveway. Ed flung the front door open and walked outside when he saw Jason pull up.

"Now Ed, I want you to calm down. I’m going to stay over here with you tonight, and we’ll drive to Columbus first thing in the morning. You need to be sober when you confront Chris." Jason said as he got out of the car.

"No way! You'll take me to my wife right now, or I'll drive myself!" Ed yelled as he grabbed Jason up by the collar of his shirt and slammed him up against the car.

"Ok chill man. Let's go!" Jason replied.

As Jason drove Ed to Columbus, Georgia, Ed yelled and cursed and made horrible threats the entire ride. When they finally reached the hotel, Ed jumped out of the car and rushed into the lobby, and up to the receptionist.

"Do you have a Leslie Johnson here?" Ed slurred.

"Sorry sir, but we can't give out that information." The neatly dressed clerk said as he reached under his desk and pushed the security button.

"Fine no problem, I'll look for her myself. Come on Jason!" Ed said as he took long strides to the elevator and pushed the up button.

Chapter10

"I'll be right back, I'm going down to the lobby to request more wash cloths from room service," Chris said as he headed toward the door.

"Why don't you just call the front desk?" Leslie asked.

"Something's wrong with the phone," Chris replied before leaving the room. Chris got onto the elevator and went down 29 floors to the first floor.

As the elevator door opened, Ed stared straight into the face of the man who was trying to steal his wife. As soon as Ed saw Chris he punched him in the face. The force of the blow caught Chris by surprise and sent him to the floor. Chris jumped up only to be punched again.

"Motherfucker where's my wife! I told you to stay the fuck away from her!" Ed yelled with rage. Chris fell again but managed to scramble up from the floor, push past Ed, and began running down the hallway. Ed ran after Chris and tackled him like a football player, sending both of them flying to the floor. Somehow, Chris managed to get the better of Ed, he jumped on top of Ed and began swinging, punching Ed in the face and head. Jason ran over to them, and sucker punched Chris to get him off Ed, causing Chris to fly backward. Ed jumped up. Both men ran over to Chris and began kicking him. Chris threw his hands over his head to protect it from the vicious kicks. Blood was everywhere. All the commotion brought everyone out into the lobby.

Leslie had decided to follow Chris down to the lobby because she wanted to ask for more coffee. When Leslie reached the lobby and got off the other elevator, she screamed when she saw her husband and his friend attacking Chris. She ran over to them.

"Ed! Jason! Stop it!" She screamed as she ran over to Chris. Ed and Jason stopped kicking Chris when Leslie jumped in front of them. Leslie bent down to help Chris stand back up. Ed furiously walked over to Leslie with the look of Satan on his face.

"What the fuck are you doing here with him? You've been cheating on me with this motherfucker?" Ed yelled as he grabbed Leslie's arm. Chris attacked Ed, punching him in his face.

"Keep your hands off her!" Chris screamed. Jason was about to swing on Chris again when the hotel security followed by the police ran over to them and broke up the fight. The police grabbed all three men.

"How could you do this to me! How could you betray me like this? You're my wife; I love you Leslie!" Ed screamed at Leslie with tears running down his face as a policeman put handcuffs on him.

"You have the nerve to ask me that! This is all your fucking fault you cheating bastard! You introduced me to him! You wanted me to fuck him, remember? This is all your fucking fault Ed!" Leslie screamed as she started crying.

"Your days are numbered you sorry Bitch!" Chris yelled at Ed as the police escorted the handcuffed men toward the front entrance. Chris's words sent Ed into a rage.

"Are you threatening me Motherfucker?" Ed screamed as he struggled to break free from the police officers. Leslie jumped back on the elevator and ran into her hotel room, throwing herself on the bed.

"Oh my God, what have I done?" Leslie sobbed uncontrollably.

Ed, Jason, and Chris were all taken to the police station in separate cars. Ed couldn't get Leslie's words out of his head. "It's your fault!" She had screamed. Ed knew she was right. If he hadn't insisted on her going to that swinger's club with him, she would've never met Chris. He was so hurt. He knew he had just lost the most important person in his life. Ed moved around in the back seat of the police car trying to get comfortable. His arms were starting to feel numb from the tight handcuffs. When they finally reached the police station, Ed was escorted to a cell filled with twenty other men. Jason and Chris were placed in different jail cells.

Ed figured he'd make bail before morning since it wasn't a serious charge. But after being in jail for more than twelve hours his world was turned upside down. A deputy informed him that he wouldn't be getting out of jail because there was a warrant out for his arrest and instead he was being transferred to Fulton County Jail in Atlanta, Georgia.

"A warrant for what!" Ed yelled at the deputy.

"Looks like you're being charged with the murder of a woman named Tammy Morrison." The deputy replied. Ed almost fell out. Tammy was dead?

"What!" Ed screamed.

"Yep looks like they charged you with the murder this morning."

"But I didn't kill her!" Ed screamed.

"Yea, that's what they all say. Tell it to the judge," the deputy said sarcastically before walking away from the cell.

Ed walked into the common area and sat down on the iron bench. Was this some type of nightmare? He asked himself. Another inmate walked up to the television and turned the channels until he found the local news channel. Ed gasped when he saw his face flash across the screen along with pictures of the crime scene.

"Officials have informed us that Tammy Morrison's body was discovered at this apartment complex last night. Edward Johnson Jr. is currently in custody in Columbus, Georgia on an unrelated charge. He is being charged with the murder of his mistress and will be transported back to Atlanta. Sergeant Maloney has informed us that the prosecution made the decision to charge Mr. Johnson after several witnesses who live in the neighborhood stated they heard and saw Mr. Johnson arguing with Ms. Morrison the same day her body was discovered. Edward Johnson Jr. is the son of Edward Johnson SR, one of the most influential and highly respected law firm CEO's in Atlanta." The news reporter stated as he pointed towards Tammy's apartment. Ed was in shock. He had only stopped by Tammy's house to beg her to have an abortion. She had gotten mad at him and grabbed a butcher knife threatening to stab him. He had grabbed the knife from her and threw it across the room before storming out of the house and driving home. She was alive when he left. Someone else must have killed her. But who? He asked himself.

Chapter 11

Mia sat in the police station waiting area, waiting for Chris to walk through the door. He smiled when he saw her.

"Thanks for bailing me out," he stated as he walked over to her and gave her a hug.

"It's been all over the news. Ed's being held without a bond for murder," Mia said as they walked out of the police station.

"Really? Well good for him." Chris chuckled. "Listen, I need you to take me back to the hotel. I need to get my car," Chris stated as he got in her car. Mia drove Chris back to the resort.

"Do you need me to follow you back to Atlanta?" She asked.

"No, I'm going to see Leslie first," Chris said as he got out of the car.

"Okay, see you later," Mia waved as she drove off. Chris walked into the hotel and rode the elevator up to Leslie's room. Leslie hugged Chris as soon as she opened the door.

"Are you okay?" She asked as she stepped aside and allowed him to enter the room. She walked over to him and began inspecting the bruises on his face.

"Yea, I'm fine. Have you been watching the news? Your husband has been charged with murdering his ex-lover."

"What?" Leslie yelled in shock. She ran over to the bed and picked up the remote control, turning the television to Channel 5.

"Yea, they say his fingerprints were all over the murder weapon and that neighbors saw him leaving her place," Chris said as he walked into the bathroom and looked in the mirror to inspect the bruises on his face.

"I don't believe it. My husband is a lot of things but he's not a murderer," Leslie said shaking her head in disbelief as she continued to turn the channels on the television, searching for more news coverage about her husband.

"Well maybe you don't know him as well as you think," Chris replied. Leslie stood up and walked over to her cell phone, she picked it up and dialed Jason's number.

"Hello," Jason answered.

"Jason, its Leslie, please tell me what's going on with Ed," She begged.

"Well, it looks like they found a woman named Tammy Morrison murdered in her home and they're accusing Ed of killing her. But I know he didn't do it. Don't worry Leslie, I'm going to find out who the real killer is."

"I'm coming back to Atlanta today. I want to speak with his father about getting him a good lawyer. I'll call you when I get there," Leslie stated.

"Okay but there's no need to rush back. I have an appointment set up with Ed's dad," Jason said calmly.

"Thank you, Jason, you're such a good friend," Leslie stated before ending the call.

"Why are you so worried about him? You're divorcing him remember? At least he's out of the way and won't come between you and me," Chris said as he walked over to her and pulled her into his arms. He tried to kiss her, but Leslie pulled away.

"We aren't divorced yet and he needs me. I know in my heart that he didn't do this," Leslie said as she walked over to the closet, pulled out her suitcase, and began packing. Chris walked over to Leslie and pulled her back into his arms again.

"Ed doesn't deserve you. Don't worry about him right now. Let's enjoy each other." He said as he kissed her passionately. Leslie pulled away again.

"You're right, he doesn't deserve me. But he needs me right now. I'm sorry Chris but I need to be there for him," Leslie said as she began packing again.

Mia was deep in thought as she drove the two and a half hours back to Atlanta. Although she was forced to remain loyal to Chris, her heart went out to Ed. She had really started liking him. Plus, he was a much better lover than Chris. Mia thought to herself as she remembered their last time together. Mia loved performing oral sex. She loved the feel and taste of a man's dick in her mouth. It did something to her to watch the men jump around. It made her feel powerful. Chris never liked oral sex, which Mia had always thought was weird. But Ed loved it.

Mia had met Chris years ago in Las Vegas when she was a heroin addicted seventeen-year-old prostitute. Her parents had been killed in a car accident when Mia was only 7 years old. After their death, she lived with her grandmother until she died from a heart attack when Mia was 12. With no one in the family willing to take on the responsibility of raising a rebellious teenager, Mia was shuffled around from one foster home to the next. She got tired of being mistreated by the women and molested by the men in the various foster homes, so at 15 she became a runaway. Mia quickly learned that the only way to survive in the streets was to sell her body. Her first pimp got her hooked on Heroin.

The night Chris picked her up on the strip, Mia had been fascinated with his ruggedly handsome looks and his wealth. Even though Chris wasn't the greatest lover in the world, Mia instantly fell in love with him because of how he treated her. She begged Chris to let her stay with him because her pimp was abusive, and she was tired of the street life. He agreed, and she became his mistress.

Mia's pimp found her a few weeks later while she was walking to the grocery store that was three blocks from Chris's condo. When Mia refused to leave with him he attacked her, almost killing her and leaving her in an alley for dead. Fortunately, a business owner who was emptying his trash in the alley found her and called 911.

When Chris found out what happened. He promised Mia that he would take care of it and she would never have to worry about her pimp again. Two weeks later, the police found her pimp in a warehouse, beaten to death with his tongue cut out, and two bullet holes in his head. From that moment on Mia felt indebted to Chris and promised that she would always be loyal to him. Eventually Chris began to trust Mia and involve her with his drug dealings with the Mafia, Casino dealings, and ordered hits on people who didn't pay their debts. She also helped run his legitimate businesses. Mia had become his right-hand woman. Whatever he needed done she did it.

Last year, Chris decided he wanted to expand his enterprise into the Atlanta, Georgia area and get into the real-estate and entertainment business. He began making trips to Atlanta, buying commercial property and opening recording studios. The night they met Ed and his wife, Chris told Mia that he had a new business contact who had invited him to meet him at Tiger’s. Chris told her that Tigers was a swinger's club and that she was going to play his wife. They had visited lots of swinger's clubs in Las Vegas and had some awesome sexual experiences with other couples in the past, so Mia had been excited.

When Chris first told Mia about his plan to get revenge against Ed, Mia had agreed without hesitation. She figured something must have gone wrong with their business deals that had Chris upset. Mia never asked questions, she just obeyed orders. When Chris started paying Leslie so much attention, initially Mia had been jealous. What was so special about Leslie? Mia didn't even think she was all that cute. Why couldn't Chris look at her like that? Why couldn't he love her the way she had always loved him. Mia was the one who had always been there for Chris not Leslie. Why couldn't he see that? She often wondered.

Mia pulled her car into her drive way, got out of the car, and walked into her house. When she walked into the living room she saw the light on her answering machine blinking. She walked over to the desk and pushed the button to check her messages. She had missed a call from Fulton County Jail. Mia knew Ed was trying to call her. She began walking towards the kitchen when the house phone began ringing. Mia ran back over to the phone and saw Fulton County Jail on the caller ID. She smiled as she picked up the phone. The operator came on the line.

"You have a collect call from an inmate at Fulton County Jail, do you accept this call? Say Yes or press 1 to accept this call. Say no or press 2 to reject this call." The operator recording stated.

"Yes, I accept." Mia was happy to hear from him.

"Hello Mia?"

"Hello Ed, are you okay?"

"Yes, I know that by now you've heard about the murder. I want you to know that I'm innocent. I didn't do it."

"I believe you," Mia replied.

"Can you come and visit me? My visitation days are Monday's and Friday's from 1p-2p."

"Sure, I'll come see you." Mia said as she carried her cordless phone into the living room and sat down on the couch. Chris had no idea that Mia was still secretly seeing Ed. He probably would've flipped out and called her a traitor if he knew.

"When you come, wear a mini skirt and don't wear any underwear," Ed stated.

"Okay. What's today Tuesday? I'll come on Friday."

"Okay, I'll see you on Friday talk to you later," Ed replied before hanging up the phone.

"Alright Johnson, if you're finished with your call you can go back to your cell," a male officer stated. Ed walked away from the payphone and back towards his cell as the next inmate in line made a call. He took a backward glance at the payphone as he thought about Leslie. He should have tried to call her, but he wasn't sure if she would accept his call after what happened at the hotel. He wondered if she knew about the murder. Did she think he did it? He asked himself as he walked up the steel steps toward his cell. Ed was deep in thought and didn't realize that two female officers were staring at his physique as he walked up the steps.

"My, I see we have fresh meat in the building," officer Latham whispered as she eyed Ed.

"Yea, and he's too fine. I bet he has a big dick," officer Brown giggled softly.

Ed was asleep when officer Latham and officer Brown walked into his cell in the wee hours of the morning.

"Johnson, get up and follow us." They demanded as they stood next to his bunk.

"Where am I going?" He asked as he jumped off the top bunk and put on his jail issued flip flops. The officers walked out of his cell without answering. Ed's cell mate shook his head as he watched the officers lead Ed down the steps. He already knew where the officers were taking him.

"Lucky bastard," his cell mate mumbled as he turned over in the bed and went back to sleep.

Ed followed the officers down a dark hallway and into an interrogation room.

"Sit down!" Officer Brown ordered as she pointed toward a yellow chair sitting next to a table. Ed wondered why they were going to interrogate him in the middle of the night. When officer Latham locked the door and officer Brown began to pull down his pants, he realized that he wasn't about to be interrogated, he was about to be seduced. Officer Brown got down on her knees in front of Ed and freed his limp manhood from his orange jump suit. She tore open a condom and slid it on before placing his manhood in her mouth. She began sucking as officer Latham began kissing him. It didn't take long for Ed's manhood to become erect.

"Looks like our little friend's excited," officer Brown giggled as she began massaging his penis with her hand before putting his erect manhood back into her mouth. Ed couldn't stop the moan that escaped his lips as officer Brown began sucking. She placed her tongue on the top of his penis and began circling it as she continued to massage the lower part of his manhood with her hand. Officer Latham walked out of the room and returned a few minutes later with two blankets and a pillow. She laid the blankets onto the floor.

"Take off your jump suit and lay down," officer Latham ordered as she pointed toward the blankets. Officer Brown released Ed, allowing him to follow the orders. Once Ed was on the blanket, officer Latham and officer Brown got undressed. Officer Latham straddled Ed's face in between her legs and officer Brown laid down in between his legs and placed his dick back in her mouth.

"Suck me," officer Latham ordered. Ed wasted no time allowing his tongue to find its way into her womanhood. He listened to her moan as he began to suck on her clitoris. Once officer Latham reached an orgasm, she switched places with officer Brown.

"I want you to do to me what you just did to her," officer Brown growled. Ed moaned as he did as he was ordered. He couldn't concentrate on pleasing officer Brown as much because officer Latham was doing things to his penis and testicles that no other woman had ever done before. Her oral sex skills were much better than the other officer. He felt officer Latham jump on top and begin to move up and down. Ed had always had fantasies of sleeping with two women at one time. Never in a million years did he think his fantasy would come true in jail. All three reached an orgasm at the same time. Afterward, they all got redressed.

"You'd better not say anything to anyone about this or we'll make sure you don't make it out of here alive," officer Latham warned as they lead him back to his cell.

"I see you've been officially welcomed to block 7. It was good as hell wasn't it?" His cellmate chuckled after the officers walked away.

"They did the same thing to you when you first got here?" Ed asked with a surprised look on his face.

"Yep,"

"How are they able to get away with it?" Ed asked as he jumped back on the top bunk.

"Everyone's too scared to say anything. Plus, you get better treatment when you're one of their whores," his cellmate replied. Maybe having the officers on his side could work in his favor, he thought as he allowed sleep to find him. While asleep, he began dreaming about Leslie.

Chapter 12

"I want you to come with me to Las Vegas," Chris whispered as he held Leslie's naked body in his arms.

"You want me to come to Vegas with you?" Leslie asked with raised eye brows.

"Yes, I have to fly there next week to take care of some business and I want you to come with me. You've been through a lot lately, taking a trip will help you relax. I'll make sure you have a wonderful time," Chris said as he pushed her hair away from her forehead.

"Okay, but first I want to go back to Atlanta and see Ed. I want to make sure he has good legal representation."

"Didn't you say his father owned a law firm? I'm sure he'll take care of everything."

"That's true, but I still want to see him. After all, he is still my husband," Leslie replied as she got out of the bed and walked into the bathroom.
Not for long, Chris thought to himself.

"Okay, I'll follow you back to Atlanta tomorrow. Go see him if that's going to make you feel better. But will you please come with me. I need to have you by my side," Chris said as he got out of bed. After all Ed put her through, Chris couldn't understand why she was so concerned about the motherfucker. But he knew it wouldn't be wise to push too hard.

"Okay, I'll come and stay for a little while. I guess it would be fun. I haven't been to Vegas in years," Leslie yelled from the bathroom.

"Great, we'll leave next Friday evening. You want some coffee?" Chris asked as he walked into the small kitchenette and turned on the coffee maker. Chris smiled as he thought about his plans for Leslie. He began whistling as he poured coffee grains into coffee maker.

As Leslie drove back to Atlanta, she began to think about her life. She had been so in love with Ed that she overlooked his infidelities and had compromised her own morals to try to save their marriage.

"Why am I so stupid?" She blurted out loud.

"I can't believe I'm going through all this because of this man." Frustrated, she pulled over to the side of the road and she called her oldest and dearest friend Courtney. Looking in the review mirror she saw Chris pull over behind her. She exhaled deeply when Courtney answered the phone with a chipper hello.

"Courtney, I need to talk to you, it's about Ed. Can I come over?" Leslie asked, trying not to cry.

"Sure," Courtney replied.

"Okay, I'll be there in 45 minutes," Leslie replied before ending the call and throwing her cell phone on the passenger seat before pulling back onto the road.

When they finally reached her house, Chris wanted to come inside and get a quickie. Leslie wanted to laugh when he said the word "quickie". How much quicker could sex with him be? It already didn't last more than three minutes. Leslie thought to herself as she unlocked her front door. She told him she was tired and just wanted to rest.

It was obvious from the expression on his face that Chris was disappointed, but he told her he understood. As soon as he left, Leslie jumped back into her car and drove to Courtney's house on the other side of the city. She really needed a good friend to talk to. Everything was happening too fast and crazy in her life. Leslie felt like she was in a state of confusion. She had much love and respect for Courtney, she was so smart. She always seemed to know exactly what to say to make Leslie feel better and her advice was always right on point. Leslie felt lucky to have a psychologist as a best friend because she got free professional advice.

Chris decided to keep an eye on Leslie, because he didn't trust Jason. All he needed was one of Ed's friends coming around and trying to undo all the hard work he had put in with the newly budding romance. He drove up the block, out of Leslie's view. It wasn't long before he saw her walk out of the house and jump into her car. Where's she going? Chris wondered. He followed her making sure he stayed far enough behind her, so she didn't see him.

"She better not be going to see Ed," he muttered under his breath. When she finally pulled into the driveway of a beautiful southern mansion, he watched her walk up and ring the bell. Chris was somewhat relieved that a beautiful woman, around Leslie's age, answered the door.

"Well, well. I wonder who this is. Leslie, why did you lie to me and not tell me where you were going?" Chris said out loud to himself as he lit a cigarette and inhaled deeply. His cellphone starting ringing, it was Mia.

"Hello, perfect timing. I need you to figure out who lives at 1425 Oak Tree Lane, Atlanta, Georgia," Chris said giving her a chance to speak.

"Okay I can do that... " Mia paused, "but first I need to tell you something."

"Okay, what's up?" Chris asked skeptically.

"Ed asked me to come visit him," Mia replied.

"Why would he do...wait...have you been seeing him?" Chris asked with fury building in his voice.

"Yes," Mia admitted.

"You could've ruined my entire plan!" He yelled. Chris became silent as he tried to work this new piece of information into his plan.

"When are you supposed to visit him?" He asked after a few minutes.

"Friday, from 1-2p.m," Mia replied.

"Alright go, but Leslie's going to show up too. Make sure she sees you with him and let her know that he asked you to come," Chris demanded.

"Okay," Mia replied hesitantly.

"Don't screw this up for me, Mia. You know what will happen if you do!" Chris said in a threatening tone.

"I won't!" Mia was irritated with his lack of trust.

"Call me as soon as you get the information on the address," Chris said before abruptly ending the call.

Leslie was greeted by Courtney with a smile and a hug.

"Girl it's so good to see you. I was just thinking about you yesterday," Courtney said smiling as she held the screen door open.

"I've missed you too," Leslie replied as she hugged Courtney again before walking into the house.

"Please have a seat. Would you like something to drink? I have coffee, tea, bottled water, Sprite, and orange juice," Courtney said as she walked into the kitchen.

"I'll take a glass of orange juice. I'm trying to lay off the caffeine," Leslie said as she began admiring the framed pictures of Courtney's husband and their children on the fireplace mantel.

"Okay, I can tell something's on your mind so spit it out," Courtney yelled from the kitchen.

"Your children are growing so fast. It seems like just yesterday that your son was learning how to crawl, and your daughter is going to be beautiful just like her mother." Leslie said smiling as she picked up one of the pictures of Courtney's children, ignoring Courtney's question.

"Thank you. Okay enough with the small talk, lay it on me. I've known you for twenty-five years. I know when something's wrong," Courtney said as she walked back into the living room holding a large glass of orange juice. She handed

Leslie the glass before sitting down on the couch. The look Courtney had on her face let Leslie know that she might as well just spit it out.

"I'm divorcing Ed. Have you heard about the murder on the news?" Leslie blurted out as she placed the picture back on the fireplace mantel and sat down next to Courtney on the couch.

"A divorce? You and Ed are getting a divorce? What murder? I've been so busy over the last few weeks that I haven't had time to watch television," Courtney admitted. Leslie exhaled deeply and then took a drink from her glass. Tears began to form in her eyes.

"Ed got another woman pregnant," Leslie sniffed. Immediately Courtney's heart went out to Leslie. Courtney knew about the years of cheating Leslie had to endure. She also knew about her miscarriages and childbearing problems. She knew how desperately Leslie wanted to have children. Courtney never really liked Ed. She hated how he treated her best friend. But she had always tried to tolerate him because he was Leslie's husband. Courtney reached for the Kleenex box on the coffee table and handed it to Leslie as she watched tears fall down her best friend's face.

"The worst part is that the pregnant woman was murdered and they're accusing Ed of killing her. He's being held without a bond in Fulton County jail," Leslie replied as she wiped her face with the Kleenex.

"Wow, do you think he did it? Do they have a lot of evidence against him?"

"I really don't know much about the case. I just found out he was in jail yesterday. But wait there's more."

"What?" Courtney asked with raised eyebrows.

"I met someone else. Well actually Ed introduced me to him. His name is Chris and he's so nice and handsome. He wants me to go on a trip with him to Vegas next week. I'm really starting to like him Courtney."

"Okay if that's true then why are you sitting here crying?" Courtney paused as she stared in Leslie's face, "You still love Ed, don't you?" Courtney asked with a concerned look. Leslie didn't answer instead she started crying harder. Courtney scooted closer to Leslie and put her arm around her shoulder.

"It's okay honey. It's okay to love your husband. You're supposed to. I can understand your desire for a divorce. You should've never had to endure that type of emotional abuse and betrayal from your husband. But I would take it slow with the new guy. Grabbing a rebound lover just to ease the pain doesn't usually work out well. Remember you're still married. If you were already single and you didn't still love your husband I would say go for it, but you still love Ed and right now... at this exact moment...he's still your husband. The one who will end up hurt in the end with be the rebound man, especially if you and your husband are able to work things out later." Leslie sniffed as she listened closely to every word Courtney said.

"Before you lead this new guy on, you need to make sure you really want to be with him. I mean, you're going to Vegas with him? How well do you know him? I mean you gotta be careful now days."

"I trust him," Leslie said defensively.

"I think you need to wait and make sure you're completely over Ed before you start dating someone new. Do you really believe Ed killed her?" Courtney asked. Leslie began shaking her head.

"No, I just have this feeling deep inside that he's innocent. I know this man better than his own momma. Ed is a lot of things, but I know without a doubt that he would never try to physically hurt a woman," Leslie replied.

"If you still love your husband, my advice to you would be to hold off on filing for a divorce right now. Things are too unstable, a legal separation maybe but not a divorce. Stand by your husband's side until you find out the truth. If he's innocent, this situation might be what your husband needs to make him a better man." Courtney said smiling. Leslie had to agree, everything Courtney was saying made sense. Leslie knew she still loved her husband. But she wasn't sure about leaving Chris alone. Regardless of what Courtney said, Leslie felt like she needed Chris to help her get through this and she wasn't ready or willing to end their relationship right now.

Chris sat in his car impatiently waiting for Mia to call back. Fifteen minutes passed before his phone began ringing again.

"What the hell took so long?" Chris yelled into the phone.

"You want the info or not?" Mia barked back before continuing.

"Her name is Courtney Miller. She's a psychologist in the area. I also found out she went to school with Leslie. Is there anything else you need to know?" Mia asked feeling slightly irritated.

"No, I think that's all I need to know for now," Chris answered. "I'll call you if I need anything else." Hanging up before Mia had a chance to respond, Chris stared at the house for a few more minutes before pulling off.

Chapter 13

Jason sat in a plush office admiring the many certificates and pictures that hung on the wall as he waited for Edward Johnson Sr. Ed's father walked into the room holding a cup of coffee, he was an older man in his early seventies. Ed had a lot of his father's facial features. James Patterson, one the firms top defense attorney's followed Edward Sr. into the room and took a seat next to Jason.

"Alright, what information have you two been able to gather so far?" Ed's father asked as he sat behind the large mahogany desk and took a drink from his green coffee cup.

"We're still waiting for the autopsy reports to come back. But so far, we know they have a murder weapon with only Ed and the dead woman's fingerprints on it. A next door neighbor whose name is.." James paused as he flipped through his notes, "Karen Jenkins and her husband Jim Jenkins are the prosecutor's star witnesses. They told my assistant that they heard a heated argument between the victim and Ed when they got home from a poker game the night the victim's body was discovered. They also saw Ed speed away from the victim's house that night around 7:30pm. They said they never heard or saw anyone else enter the victim's home that night," James stated as he read from a small note book.

"After our meeting today, I'm going to stop by an old friend and see if he has heard anything on the streets about the murder," Jason stated.

"Alright, well keep me informed." Ed's father began coughing.

"Are you alright sir?" Jason asked with a concerned look. That cough didn't sound good to Jason.

"Yes, I'm fine," Ed's father replied after finally catching his breathe. Jason knew that this whole situation was causing Ed's father a lot of stress. It was obvious that the stress was starting to affect his health.

After the meeting Jason drove through East Pointe, Georgia to an area that was extremely poverty stricken. He parked his car in front of an old corner grocery store. There were a few men in front of the store smoking cigarettes and drinking beer. One-dollar bills were scattered on the ground, the money was surrounded by men who were laughing and yelling as they played craps.

“Single cigarettes, Starbucks, movies, and CD’s,” a bootlegger yelled at Jason.

“No thanks man,” Jason said as he walked toward the entrance of the store. Jason waved at a couple of men he knew as he walked into the store and up to the counter.

"Hey Ted, how are you? Where's Gary?"

"Hey Jason, what's up man, haven't seen you in a while. He's in the back," Ted replied pointing to a door in the back of the store.

"Thanks man, hey what did you think about that Hawks and Bulls game last night?"

"Man, you know I'm a Grady baby, I'll always support my Atlanta teams, but I have to admit the Bulls do appear to have a good team this year."

"Man, I lost a hundred dollars on that game. I just knew Atlanta was going to smash Chicago," Jason laughed before walking toward the back of the store. When Jason reached the door he briefly knocked before entering.

"Hey Gary, what's up?" Jason asked. Gary was sitting at a desk going over the store's accounting books.

"Hey Jason." They shook hands. Gary smiled, revealing his missing two front teeth.

"Hey man, how's the wife and kids?" Jason asked as he sat down in a chair in front of the desk.

"They're all fine, you know Julie will be a freshman in college this year and Thomas just made the basketball team at his high school. Gary said proudly.

"That's awesome man."

"Martha just asked me the other day if I had heard from you," Gary said as he closed the books and lit a cigarette.

"Tell your wife I said hello and ask her to make sure you invite me to dinner the next time she makes Buffalo wings," Jason laughed.

"I sure will, so what's up with you man?" Gary asked as he took a drag from his cigarette.

"Well, you know me, always working on the next big investigation. A friend of mine is in jail, accused of murdering a young woman over on Upper Riverdale Road last week."

"I heard about that on the news."

"Yea, well I was just wondering if you could put out a word for me and see if anyone's talking on the streets."

"I sure will man. I'll call you if I find out anything. Hey Jason, how's Samantha? When are you two going to finally settle down and get married?"

"She's fine. I don't care how long we've been together, I'm not marrying her. I'll think about marriage when I find a woman worthy of my love. That woman I got is too crazy," Jason laughed. The two men continued to talk for another hour before Jason finally left the store.

Jason decided that while he was waiting for word on the streets about the murder, that he'd put in a call to his old friend at the precinct and see if they could pull up any information about this Chris fella. There was something about the last statement he made at the hotel that day of the fight that had Jason's mental antenna up on alert.

Chris had threatened Ed and told him that his days were numbered. He planned to keep a close eye on Chris Peterson. He picked up his cell phone and began dialing numbers.

Chapter 14

Leslie began to reminisce about her wedding day as she drove to the jail to see Ed that Friday afternoon. Her wedding day had been the happiest day of Leslie's life. Ed's father had spent thousands of dollars to make sure that his only son and new daughter in law had a very memorable wedding and honeymoon. Ed had made her feel like she was the most beautiful bride in the world. That night was very special because Leslie had been a virgin.

No matter how much he begged or how much they made out, Leslie had refused to go all the way with him. Sometimes Leslie wondered if withholding sex from Ed had been the right thing to do. She smiled as she remembered how gentle he had been on their honeymoon night. He started off slow, making sure that he brought her pleasure. Leslie's wedding night was also the first night she ever experienced an orgasm. She smiled as she remembered how embarrassed she'd been once the orgasmic sensation had subsided. But Ed had assured her it was alright, and it was the response he wanted. When he first entered her womanhood, it had been very painful, but after a while she couldn't help but wrap her legs around him allowing him to go deeper.

Maybe Courtney was right. Maybe going to Vegas with Chris wasn't the right thing to do. She did still love Ed. A wife's duty was to stand by her husband's side no matter what. Maybe getting a divorce wasn't the right thing to do. After all, the affair between Tammy and Ed had been months ago, it's not like he was still cheating on her. Leslie thought as she turned into the Fulton County Jail visitor parking lot. Leslie sat in the car for a moment and took a deep breath before getting out of the car. Never in her wildest dreams did she ever envision having to visit her husband in jail. Leslie thought about Chris as she got out of the car and walked toward the entrance. Chris had tried to convince her not to see Ed. She finally had to let him know that nothing he could say would stop her from going to see her husband. She cared for Chris, but Ed was her husband. Chris told her that if she was going to see him, Friday would be the best day because it probably wouldn't be crowded. When she walked into the visitation lobby she signed in and sat down as she waited to be called. She was completely caught off guard when she saw Mia walk through the door.

"What the heck is she doing here?" Leslie whispered out loud with a frown as she watched Mia walk up to the front desk wearing a very short mini shirt.

Mia noticed Leslie as soon as she walked through the door. Chris had already informed her that Leslie would be there. As Mia signed herself in she felt Leslie's eyes on her back and she couldn't help but laugh inwardly. "You have no idea what you're getting yourself into Leslie." Mia said to herself as she sat down in the lobby. Mia wasn't surprised when Leslie walked over to her.

"What're you doing here Mia?" Leslie asked boldly.

"Ed asked me to come," Mia answered calmly.

"He what!" Leslie said a little louder than she had intended.

"You heard me," Mia replied.

"Leslie Johnson!" An officer called Leslie's name, breaking Leslie's train of thought. She rolled her eyes at Mia before following the officer back to the visitation room. When Ed saw Leslie, a look of shock splashed across his face.

"You called Mia instead of me? Are you still sleeping with her?" Leslie asked when she reached him.

"You were with that guy. I didn't think you'd want to see me." Ed answered truthfully, ignoring her second question.

"So, you called Mia to comfort you, how cute. You've still been sleeping with her all this time, haven't you?" Leslie asked again. Ed didn't answer. He just couldn't bear to see the hurt on her face.

"Haven't You!" Leslie screamed! Everyone in the visitation room turned around to look at them.

"Keep your voices down!" An officer ordered. Ed stared Leslie in the face before looking away. Leslie shook her head. She didn't need Ed to admit what she already knew.

"I should've never come here!" Leslie said sarcastically as she turned to leave.

"Wait, Leslie wait, I love you!" Ed pleaded.

"Love, what could you possibly know about love? Love is faithful Ed, Love is loyal. You know nothing about love!" Leslie laughed bitterly. Leslie looked straight into Ed's eyes, "Marriage and commitment are a two-way street. I'm tired of being the only one honoring our vows Ed. I'm tired of being the only one committed to this marriage. I'm tired of giving you my heart, mind, body, and soul but receiving nothing but pain and shame in return. I'm tired of being the laughing stock of the community while you continue to sneak around behind my back. It's over Ed!" Leslie screamed before walking away. Ed put his hands over his face and moaned.

Leslie walked pass Mia without even a glance and walked out of the building.

Mia followed the police officer to the visitation room. When Mia saw Ed sitting at the table looking so handsome and rugged in his orange prison suit she felt an emotion that caught her by surprise. At that moment she realized she was beginning to fall in love with him. She'd been trying so hard not to allow love to enter the equation because she knew it would only complicate things, but she couldn't seem to help it.

Mia walked over to the table and sat down next to him. Normally this wouldn't have been allowed, but Ed did a private session with officer Brown the night before in return for the opportunity to touch Mia during visitation. Mia noticed the look of distress on Ed's face. She smiled inwardly.

"I saw Leslie in the waiting area. Are you okay?" She asked taking his hand in hers.

"Yes, I had no idea she was coming. I would've never allowed the two of you to come at the same time," Ed said as he withdrew his hand.

"I've missed you," she sighed, as she slid her hand in between his thighs to touch the hard bulge in his pants, ignoring the fact that he had just pulled away from her. Ed couldn't help himself, he slid his hands under her mini skirt. He took a deep breath when he realized she had obeyed him and wasn't wearing any underwear. Mia smiled as she felt him touch her warm and wet womanhood. His touch did something to her. She had never felt this passionate feeling for Chris. She had love for Chris, but she was falling in love with Ed.

"Open your legs wider for me," he whispered. She smiled as she obeyed his command. She looked around to make sure no one was watching them. Mia took a deep breath as she felt his finger find her clitoris.

"You smell so good. You're already wet," he whispered. He could feel his dick swelling. He looked around him to see if the guards were watching him. He noticed they had their heads turned away going over paper work. He would have to give officer Brown a special thank you later tonight. He took his hand from under her skirt and began licking his fingers.

"You taste good too," he said smiling. Mia began blushing.

"I want you to know Mia, that I didn't do it. I didn't kill Tammy," Ed pleaded with a serious look on his face.

"I believe you," Mia replied. They continued to talk until his visitation time ended. She promised Ed that she would come back to see him next Tuesday and that she would put money on his books.

As Mia walked out to her car, Leslie pulled up next to her and rolled down the window. Leslie had been waiting patiently for Mia to come outside. Mia stopped walking and put her hands on her hips as she waited to see what Leslie had to say.

She wasn't about to tolerate any disrespect from Leslie.

"You've still been sleeping with my husband all this time, haven't you?" Leslie asked.

"Are you still sleeping with mine?" Mia asked sarcastically.

"What're you talking about? You and Chris aren't really married. He told me the truth!" Leslie yelled.

"Whatever, look why are you even worried about what me and Ed are doing? You're divorcing him remember?"

"I don't care if we are divorcing, he's still my husband. Why don't you go and find your own damn husband? Maybe if you stopped being such a whore, you could get a man to marry you. You're a trifling Bitch!" Leslie screamed out the window.

Mia began walking away, she knew that if she stood there any longer she was going to snatch Leslie out of that car and kick her ass. That's really what she wanted to do anyway, but she knew she would have to deal with Chris if he found out. Chris was a wonderful and loving man as long as the woman didn't make him angry. When anger set in, Chris became a completely different man. It was as if there were two sides to him. He had no problem with beating a woman into submission if she crossed him. Mia shuttered when she thought about the last beating she received from Chris when she didn't obey him.

"Look Leslie, I'm really busy and I don't have time for your name calling. I'll talk with you later. Oh, by the way, have fun in Vegas with Chris," Mia said smiling before getting into her car and pulling off. Leslie just sat there for a moment as she watched Mia drive away.

"Fuck you Bitch!" Leslie screamed as she slammed her hand against the dashboard.

Leslie sat in the parking garage of the Hartsfield Atlanta Airport. After her experience with Mia and Ed at the jail, Leslie decided to take Chris up on his offer. She felt like a trip to Vegas is just what she needed to take her mind off her situation. She was through with Ed. She got out of the car and popped her trunk. Leslie took a deep breath as she pulled out her suitcase and began walking toward the airport entrance.

A big smile splashed across Chris's face as he watched Leslie walk down the corridor. At first, he had felt slightly apprehensive about Leslie visiting her husband in jail. He thought that if she went to see Ed, that he would talk her out of going to Vegas and encourage her to end things between them. That would have seriously damaged his plans especially since he'd already notified his contacts that she would be coming to Vegas. He knew that if she saw Mia, she would be too upset to listen to anything her husband had to say.

Obviously, Chris had been right. Seeing Mia at the jail was just what the doctor ordered. Chris chuckled as he imagined the look on Leslie's face when she saw Mia. Mia had come through once again, Chris thought to himself as he began walking toward Leslie. Chris had been planning his revenge for ten years. He had been delightfully surprised when Ed brought his wife to Tiger's that night. Chris knew Ed had a wife, but with all the different lovers in Ed's life, Leslie had seemed insignificant. Chris had assumed that he was only going to see Ed that night. His informant had already told him that Ed was a regular at the club. After meeting Leslie, Chris realized that Ed really did love his wife, and that his wife was emotionally vulnerable. At first the revenge had only included Ed, but after that night he decided that he could drive the knife even deeper by adding Leslie to the plot.

"Hello baby, I'm so glad you decided to come with me," Chris said as he kissed her softly on the lips.

"Thank you," Leslie said smiling.

"I already checked my bags in," Chris said as he took her suitcase out of her hand and began walking toward the ticket counter.

Chapter 15

Jason sat in Gary's office staring at the paper Gary had just given him with a name, number, and address written on it.

"My informant's name is Curtis. He told me there's a guy in Decatur bragging about getting paid ten thousand dollars to help set up a hit on a pregnant woman. I don't have all the details, but you might want to give Curtis a call and see what he knows."

"Thanks for the lead man," Jason said smiling. Jason recognized the address, it belonged to the Golden Gate apartments. He once had a customer who lived in those apartments on Bouldercrest. After leaving Gary's grocery store, Jason decided not to waste any time. He jumped in his car and headed toward 285 East. Once he reached the Bouldercrest exit, Jason drove to the Golden Gate apartments. It was obvious from the condition of the apartment complex that the current management was lousy. Jason drove his car through the broken gates and followed the poorly graveled road toward the back of the complex. He drove slowly until he found the building he was looking for. He pulled his car into the lot and walked up to apartment B and knocked on the door. The smell of someone frying chicken seeped through the cracks of the front door. A few seconds later a woman's voice could be heard.

"Who is it?" The woman yelled without opening the door.

"My name is Jason Patrick, I'm here to see Curtis. Gary sent me," Jason yelled back. Slowly the door opened, a fat woman with large pink rollers in her hair stood in the door way.

"Come in," she said as she stepped aside and allowed him to enter the apartment. There was a heavy-set man sitting on the couch wearing a dingy white wife beater. His chest looked like big flappy breast sitting on a big watermelon stomach. He appeared to be about sixty years old. He looked like he hadn't seen the gym or a bath in years. He acted as if he didn’t know Jason had entered the room. He continued to drink his beer as he kept his eyes glued to the small black and white television, laughing at an old episode of the Three Stooges.

"What's up Curtis, Gary said you had some information for me about the killing that happened a few weeks ago."

"How much is the information worth to you?" Curtis asked without taking his eyes off the television. Jason rolled his eyes as he dug in his pocket and pulled out two crisp twenty-dollar bills, throwing them on the coffee table. Curtis reached over and picked up the money.

"Sit down, I don't like people standing over me, it makes me nervous," Curtis said still not bothering to look at Jason. Jason sat down in a nearby chair.

"A friend of mine is friends with a member of the Black Coy gang. He said he was out with his friend at the pool hall down the street when a guy from the hood came in and bought everyone in the bar a drink. After getting drunk the guy started blabbing his mouth to my friend's friend and told him that some woman had come into the club and paid his boss a hundred thousand dollars to set up this big time lawyer. He said his boss paid him five thousand dollars to hire someone to kill the lawyer's pregnant baby momma," Curtis said before taking another swig of beer.

"Okay well, can you give me your friend's number? I want to ask him some questions." Jason stated.

"Naw, but if you give me your number I'll give it to him," Curtis said. Jason knew that the only way he was going to hear back from him was if there was something in it for him.

"Look, if you set up a meeting between me and your friend, I'll pay you two hundred dollars." Jason said as he pulled out a business card and handed it to him. Curtis looked up at Jason and started smiling, showing off his mouth full of missing teeth.

"Make it three hundred and you've got yourself a deal," he said as he reached over and snatched the card.

"Alright, make it happen within 24 hours and I'll throw in another hundred," Jason stated as he stood up and walked toward the front door.

"Alright, you'll be hearing from me by tomorrow night," Curtis yelled as Jason walked out the door.

Ed was sitting at the table in the mess hall eating with his cellmate when another inmate carrying a tray approached him.

"Hey man, I know you don't know me, but I just want to warn you that word is getting out that you're the lawyer that caused a few of the guys in here to get put away. I advise you to watch your back," he said before walking away. Ed looked around to see if anyone was watching him before returning his attention to his meal.

Over the last few weeks no one had bothered him, but he had noticed a few guys staring at him. Ed was no fool, he knew he needed protection. He decided to talk to officer Brown about it when they had their special session tonight. He could tell officer Brown was starting to fall hard for him, so getting her to arrange getting him out of general population shouldn't be difficult. He thought about Leslie, he wondered if he should try to write her a letter.

After chow Ed was walking back to his cell when a group of inmates approached him. His first thought was to run. They stopped directly in front of him, blocking his path back to his cell. A tall muscle bound man who appeared to be the leader walked up to him.

"Hey, aren't you Ed the lawyer?" The inmate asked.

"Yes, my name is Edward and yes I am a lawyer. Why?" Ed tried his best to look tough even though inside he was scared as hell. He shivered as his mind drifted to the horror stories he heard about prison.

"My name is Pedro. You must have some friends in high places who really like you. Me and my people are being paid good money to protect you while you're here. If anything goes down just let us know. I was told to give you this note," Pedro said as he handed Ed a piece of paper.

"I got my guys on 24-hour watch, you don't need to worry about anything. We know there was a few guys who were about to start some drama, but we handled that this morning," Pedro said before walking back toward the group of inmates. Everyone in the group looked like they weighed 250 pounds or more and were professional wrestlers. Ed had heard about a big fight this morning that sent four inmates to the hospital.

"Thanks," Ed mumbled as he walked past the group and up to his cell block. Once he reached his cell he sat down on his bunk and opened the piece of paper the inmate had given him. He read the note to himself.

"I love you, don't worry I'm going to get you out...Mia." Ed sat back against the wall in shock. Mia had hired inmates to protect him?

For the next few days, Ed sat in his cell continually trying to come up with answers to the questions that had been filling his mind. “How had Mia known I needed protection, and how did she have the resources to get it for me?" He asked himself. He knew the answers to his questions couldn't be good.

Chapter 16

Leslie took a deep breath as she stood in the shower. The hot water splashing against her skin felt soothing. It had been almost a week since she arrived in Las Vegas with Chris. He had been such a gentleman and spared no expense to make sure she was comfortable. She tried her best not to think about Ed and Mia. After taking her shower she quickly put on the plush white terry cloth robe Chris had given her. She walked out of the bathroom and into the main living area of the Hyatt hotel suite. Chris told her he had some business to attend to this morning and wouldn't be back until later in the afternoon. Leslie walked into the small kitchenette and poured herself a cup of coffee. The silence in the room was interrupted by the sound of her cellphone ringing. She picked up the phone and smiled when she saw the incoming call from her mother.

"Hey mom," Leslie answered cheerfully.

"Hello dear, just wanted to call and check on you. How's your trip going so far?"

` "Fine, Chris took me to Caesar's Palace yesterday to see a show. I'm really enjoying myself."

"That's good, how's Chris doing?" Her mother asked. Leslie pushed the speaker button on her phone before placing the phone on the table.

"He's fine. He isn't here right now because he had some business to take care of today. When he gets back we're going to take a trip to Phoenix."

Suddenly, there was a knock on the door.

"Hold on mom, someone's at the door." Leslie said as she walked over to the door.

"Who is it?" Leslie asked peeking through the peep hole. There were two men standing at the door dressed in housekeeping attire with a large laundry crate.

"Housekeeping, we came to give you fresh linen and take your dirty ones."

"Okay hold on," Leslie walked away from the door.

"Hold on mom, housekeeping is here for the dirty linen," Leslie yelled toward the phone.

"No problem dear take your time. What hotel are you staying at?" Her mom asked through the cellphone speaker.

"The Hyatt, it's so beautiful, I wish you could be here to see it." Leslie said as she walked into the bathroom. She grabbed all her dirty towels and walked back to the front door. When she opened the door the two men pushed the laundry crate into the room. One of the men took the dirty towels from her and handed her the clean linen.

"Thank you so much, hold on let me give you a tip," Leslie said as she took the towels. She didn't realize that one of the men had closed the door. She also didn't notice the man that walked up behind her until she turned around. She didn't get a chance to speak before the man grabbed her and covered her mouth with a small white hand towel. She began to scream and try to fight him before the odorless substance on the towel caused her to black out. Once unconscious she fell limp in the man's arms.

"Bring the crate over here so I can put her in it," the man holding Leslie yelled to his accomplice.

"Leslie, are you okay? What's going on in there?" Her mother screamed after hearing the commotion. The accomplice pushed the crate over to his partner before walking over to the table and picking up the cellphone.

"Sorry, but Leslie's busy right now," His accomplice said in a heavy Russian accent before ending the call and throwing the cellphone back on the table. After they put Leslie's body in the crate, they pulled the flap over the crate and pushed it out of the hotel room.

Leslie felt groggy as she slowly opened her eyes. It appeared that she was lying in a bed in some type of dark room. There were no windows in the room. She couldn't tell if it was day or night. She noticed that her hands and feet were tied together with a rope and she had tape over her mouth. Her eyes grew wide as she remembered the two men who had kidnapped her. She started jerking around, struggling to free her hands from the rope when she noticed a movement out the corner of her eye. A large man began walking toward her.

"I see sleeping beauty has finally awakened." The man said with a deep accent as he kneeled beside her and began stroking her hair. Leslie started screaming but all that could be heard through the tape on her mouth were muffled sounds. The fear in her eyes told it all.

"I've been waiting for you to wake up," he chuckled as he ran his fingers down her thigh. Leslie began jerking her body trying to scoot away from the kidnaper's prying fingers. He smiled as he watched her wiggle away, a twinkle of mischief glowing in his eyes. He stood up and grabbed her tied ankles toward him. He took out a knife and cut the rope. Leslie immediately starting kicking, trying to keep him from getting any closer. But the kidnapper managed to grab her by her ankles and pull her toward him as he put one knee on the bed.

"I love when they fight," the kidnapper chuckled. Suddenly the door to the room swung open and a large man entered the room.

"Jose release her! We've been ordered not to touch her before she's shipped out," the large man yelled with a heavy accent.

"Oh, I was just having a little fun boss. I wasn't going to hurt her," Jose said as he got off the bed and released his grasp on her legs. The large man walked closer to the bed and looked down at Leslie, this allowed Leslie to get a good look at him. Even in her fear, she had to admit that he was very handsome in a rugged type of way. He leaned down and began removing the tape from her mouth.

"I will remove the tape from your mouth if you promise not to scream. If you scream you will leave us no choice but to keep your mouth taped shut. Do you understand?" The large man asked. Leslie shook her head yes. But as soon as he removed the tape from her mouth, Leslie let out a loud scream and started shaking her head vigorously so that he couldn't easily re-tape her mouth. After a small struggle, her mouth was re-taped shut.

"Okay I see you're not ready to have your mouth free yet. We'll try it again later. You listen, and I'll talk. You will not be harmed. You've been bought for a very handsome price and you're being shipped overseas to your new master within the next few weeks. I know you must be hungry so when you're ready to have the tape removed without screaming, we'll feed you and give you something to drink," the large man turned around and looked at the man named Jose with a very serious look on his face.

"Inform your men that she is not to be touched. The buyer has informed us that if she's damaged in any way that he will not pay for her. If any man causes us to lose money, they will pay with the loss of their life!" The large man didn't wait for Jose to respond before walking out the door. Jose looked back at Leslie for a moment before following the large man out the door, closing and locking it behind him. Leslie laid on the bed in utter disbelief. Did she really hear him say a master had bought her and she was being shipped overseas? Tears began to slide down her face.

"Chris please come save me," her mind screamed as she rolled onto her side and drew her knees up to her chest.

Chris smiled as he boarded the airplane back to Atlanta. He found his window seat and sat down. Ed was in jail facing murder charges and Leslie had been sold to a sex slave trafficker and was on her way to Russia. He had finally carried through with his plan for revenge and the promise he made to his mother on her death bed. Chris always believed his mother had died from a broken heart. She never got over his sister's suicide. Chris could still hear his mother crying on the phone when she called to tell him that Mary had killed herself after being jilted by a married lawyer named Edward Johnson Jr. Chris had been living in Las Vegas at the time his sister was dating Ed and never got a chance to meet him.

After his sister's death, his mother fell into a deep depression and refused to eat. She grew very weak and within 6 months of his sister's suicide, his mother had a stroke and died. Chris promised that he would get revenge.

Chris pulled his cell phone out of his carryon bag and dialed Mia's number.

"Hello," Mia answered.

"It's done, I'm on my way back to Atlanta."

"She's already been shipped overseas?" Mia asked smiling.

“Yep, listen we’re about to take off. I'll call you when I reach Atlanta."

"Okay, see you when you get here," Mia said before ending the call. She smiled as she pulled the tab on her Coke and took a drink. Now that Leslie was out of the way, Ed would be all hers. She just had to figure out how she could get the charges against Ed dropped without Chris finding out.

Chapter 17

Even though Leslie was blindfolded, she could tell she was in some type of aircraft. She felt like she'd been on the aircraft for many hours. She thought about Ed, Chris, her family, and her friends. Would she ever see them again? She heard her kidnapper say that someone had paid a lot of money for her. She wondered who? Leslie felt her stomach begin to churn and her ears pop as the aircraft began descending. All thoughts beyond survival were pushed aside as strong hands gripped her arm.

"Get up!" A gruff voice said as her body was unwillingly yanked vertically. She was dragged off the plane and into a waiting car. The driver yanked off her blind fold and tape before getting in the driver's seat. The beautiful scenery of the Las Vegas Stripe had been replaced by a country side view of mountains, trees, and dirt roads. After several hours of riding, she was yanked out of the car and through the woods toward a small cabin that she could tell had a wood burning stove or fireplace by the smoky scent of oak in the air.

"Where are we?" She dared ask, her voice rough with unease and her throat parched for water. Leslie tried to get a sense of her bearings, but it was almost impossible. She'd been overseas many times, and she never forget the way it made her feel every time she saw those particularly lovely shades of green. The man who was unceremoniously hauling her toward the cabin stopped at the door and knocked three times, his log sized fists nearly causing the rafters to shake. When a tiny little granny opened the door, Leslie gasped as the woman stepped aside and said,

"Bring her inside and be quick about it!"

The man, Leslie had yet to identify, sat her roughly in a chair by the fire and retreated to what looked to be a small kitchen, where two old women stood holding a steaming cup of coffee. Leslie's stomach growled and cramped as her body began to beg for food and drink. Her mouth watered at the smell of fresh coffee. She could hear them whispering, but neither of them looked her way, and she dared not move. Her muscles screamed as her arms stayed locked behind her, handcuffed and cold. She shivered and winced with each movement. When the man once again headed toward her, she closed her eyes as she was once again jerked to a standing position.

"Time for bed darling." The little granny said as Leslie was pulled toward a small bedroom off the tiny kitchen. When her hands were finally released from the handcuffs, her arms fell to her sides, she nearly wept from the pain. She was unceremoniously stripped of her clothing and given a thin nightgown to dress in. The one kindness shown to her was a warm bath that was drawn for her. Leslie sank deep into the hot water, her muscles grateful for the almost instant relief. She closed her eyes, willing her mind to take her away from the prying eyes of her captors. With deep concentration she brought Ed's face to her mind.

His smile was genuine, and his eyes glittered with mirth as he headed toward her. She turned and ran, giggling as he chased her. Once she was caught, Ed's mouth was avid against her skin, leaving hot streaks across her neck and collar bone.

"I love you," he said breathlessly as his hands roamed over her soft breasts. They trailed down her slim torso and found the

sweet wetness. She shivered when his fingers expertly found the source of her warmth.

"I love you too," Leslie said as her body awoke to the sensations Ed stirred in her with merely a look. The thought of Ed brought waves of mixed emotions. She hated him and herself for the weaknesses he brought out. She couldn't stop the memories that flooded her mind and her body as the warm water lapped against her skin. The cuts from the handcuffs pulsed as her body remembered all too well just how Ed could make her feel, even as her mind cursed him for his infidelity.

"I need you baby," Ed said as his breath tickled Leslie's ear. His hands were still roaming over her breasts and hips as she started to grind her ass against his body, already vividly feeling his erection.

"Then take me!" Leslie said, as she felt Ed lean her over the kitchen table. She felt his fingers dig deep into her warm center, probing her until breathless moans escaped her lips. Within seconds he was inside of her, pushing her toward a climax that rocked her body with waves of pleasure.

Leslie's daydream was abruptly interrupted as the tiny granny, two men carrying rifles, and two other ladies dressed in plain brown dresses who appeared to be servants, walked into the bathroom carrying a bath towel, and a large basket full of lotions, perfumes, and a silk nightgown with a matching rob.

"Come on princess, let us help you get ready for bed. You have a long journey ahead of you tomorrow. The palace is at least a week's travel away. Master wants you there in time for the ceremony," the granny said as the other two ladies walked over to the tub and helped Leslie get out.

"My family and the authorities will be looking for me soon. I advise you to release me and send me home immediately!" Leslie demanded as she snatched the towel from one of the servants. The women ignored Leslie as they began rubbing lotion on her body.

"You might as well forget about your old life in America. You're about to have a new life as one of the wives of Prince Abacus," the old lady exclaimed proudly.

"What!" Leslie screamed in disbelief. Abacus where in the hell had she heard that name before? She racked her tired mind to any slip of information about the name that she could remember. Leslie was lead into a bedroom where she was dressed, primped, and fussed over for over an hour.

"The prince won't be happy if she isn't perfect," one of the ladies in brown said.

"And it'll be our asses on the line for it," another lady chimed in.

Leslie tried hard to hide her discontent and fear as her hair was toyed with until is shone like dark mahogany. It was intricately piled atop her head with a wavy strand flowing down her back. Her makeup was subtle as was her perfume. Her feet were adorned with simple sandals and her robe flowed lightly with each movement.

"Sit still child or this'll start to hurt!" The old lady yelled.

"I know this doesn't seem to matter to anyone here, so I'll just say it, ya'll are fucked when my family finds me!" Leslie yelled as her head was jerked backward. The old granny looked in the mirror and smiled at Leslie, making Leslie's stomach lurch.

"Your family won't find you dear. A person can quickly get lost in the sands of Saudi Arabia." Leslie jerked as the woman's bony fingers tied tiny little rose buds into her hair. Leslie felt a since of hopelessness. She knew the old lady was right, how could anyone possibly find her in Saudi Arabia?

Chapter 18

"You have a visitor!" The guard yelled through the cell bars as the cell door opened. Ed jumped up and followed the officer out of the cell toward the visitation room. Ed smiled when he saw Jason and his father sitting at the visitation table.

"Hello Dad," Ed said as he hugged his father. Ed noticed his father wasn't smiling. The look on his father's face concerned him. Ed knew something was wrong.

"What's up Jason?" Ed asked as they shook hands.

"I have some bad news to tell you. I'm not really sure how to tell you this," Jason said shaking his head.

"Man, just say it. What's wrong?" Ed asked frowning.

"Someone has kidnapped Leslie," his father blurted out.

"What?" Ed yelled jumping up from his seat.

"Sit down or your visitation time will end!" An officer barked. Ed slowly sat back down in the chair.

"She went on a trip to Las Vegas with Chris. She was on the phone talking to her mother when men disguised as housekeepers kidnapped her. Her mother said that one of the kidnappers had a foreign accent."

"Oh my God!" Ed yelled out.

"I also found out that you were set up by a woman. A gang member told me that a woman met with his friend and paid him a lot of money to kill Tammy. We had the police pick the guy up for questioning. After hours of interrogation and a bargaining deal, the guy has agreed to testify. Your lawyer is working on getting you before the judge due to this new evidence," Jason said as he glanced at his watch.

"Oh my God, somebody kidnapped my baby! You guys have got to get me out of here! I have got to find my wife!" Ed sobbed.

"Is there anyone from your past that might have wanted revenge against you?" Jason asked.

Ed knew that he had hurt so many women over the years and put so many criminals behind bars, there was no telling. The first person that came to his mind was Tammy, but since she was dead he knew that couldn't have been possible. Who hated him enough to do this? His mind went blank.

"I don't know?" Ed answered honestly.

"Well you need to think hard because that person is probably the key," Jason replied.

"So, where's Chris? Where was Chris when she was kidnapped?"

"They're holding him at the Atlanta police station to be transported back to Vegas tomorrow for questioning. I'll be flying down to Vegas tomorrow with your father. I have a friend who works for the Vegas police department so they're going to allow me to sit in for the interrogation. We'll keep you posted on the progress," Jason stated as he and Ed's father stood up. Ed stood up too as a guard walked over to him, ready to escort him back to his cell.

"Don't worry son, we're going to get you out of here," Ed's dad promised. Ed didn't say anything. He walked away from the visitation booth with slumped shoulders. He had never felt this way before. He felt like he was less than a man, he felt helpless. Someone had kidnapped his wife. Someone was trying to destroy his life and there was nothing he could do about it.

Ed walked back to his cell and sat down on the bed. His cellmate let out a loud snort before exhaling deeply. He was snoring so loud, Ed bet the entire west wing could hear him. Ed looked at the pictures of him and Leslie he had taped to the wall. He smiled as he ran his fingertips over one of the photographs of them at the park. He still remembered the day they took that picture. It was the first picture they had taken together. His heart felt like it was swelling in his chest.

Ed sat down on his bunk and began crying. Leslie was in trouble and there was nothing he could do about. All he could do was pray that she was still alive. Who would want to kidnap Leslie? Better yet, who paid gang members to kill Tammy?

Jason walked into the district attorney's office holding a large manila envelope. He walked up to a beautiful, young female receptionist sitting behind the desk and smiled.

"Hello sir, how may I help you?" She asked.

"I have a nine o'clock appointment with Mr. Fallen," Jason said smiling.

"Your name please?"

"I'm Jason Patrick with J & P Private Investigations."

"Okay, just one moment please." The receptionist replied as she typed his name into the computer.

"Okay, I've logged your arrival Mr. Patrick. Please have a seat, Mr. Fallen will be with you shortly."

"Thanks, oh by the way, I love the color of your blouse, it brings out the warmth in your beautiful eyes," Jason said smiling. He was in a good mood this morning. He knew that after this meeting with the prosecutor, all charges would have to be dropped against Ed.

"Thank you," the receptionist giggled with a big smile that seemed to stretch from ear to ear. Jason sat down in one of the visitation chairs and exhaled deeply as he picked up a Fortune 500 magazine. He was still a little tired after his trip to Vegas. He was able to get into the hotel room that Leslie had stayed in and dust for fingerprints, talk to the housekeeping staff, as well as get a copy of all the hotel surveillance tapes before going to the Las Vegas police station to sit in on Chris's interrogation. Chris had an alibi and proof that he was at the Vegas Airport at the time Leslie was abducted according to the time Leslie's mother stated she was abducted, Leslie's cell phone records, airport surveillance, and Delta passenger records. When asked why he left Leslie in Vegas while he traveled back to Atlanta, he stated he had a business conference he was scheduled to attend and had proof of his return plane ticket to Vegas after the conference ended. The police checked out his story and found out it appeared to be true. According to records he had registered for the conference months earlier. Due to lack of evidence, they had to let him go.

When Jason returned to Atlanta he sent the finger prints sent off to the forensic lab. After he finished with his meeting today, he planned to analyze the surveillance tape. A tall slender man with a receding hairline, wearing a pin stripped business suit walked into the lobby.

"Mr. Patrick," the man announced.

"Yes, that's me," Jason said as he stood up and walked over to him.

"Hello, I'm Mr. Fallen, can you follow me please?" He said after shaking Jason's hand. Jason followed the prosecutor to his office. Jason smiled as he admired the framed pictures of the prosecutor's family that were sitting on his desk.

"Please have a seat, how can I help you sir?" Mr. Fallen said as he sat down behind a large mahogany desk and pulled a piece of peppermint flavored gum out of a wrapper, popping it into his mouth.

"I have evidence that Edward Johnson Jr. did not kill Tammy Morrison. I have the names, addresses, phone numbers, and photos of witnesses and the names of the actual killers. I also have audio tapes with the recorded statements of five witnesses that all say that one of the killers was in a sports bar a few days after the murder. He was sloppy drunk and bragging about his boss getting paid thousands of dollars by an unknown woman to kill Tammy. The suspect is currently in custody and has confessed to his part of the murder plot and is willing to testify against the other members of his gang in exchange for a deal. We have also just discovered that Ed's wife has been kidnapped." Jason said as he slid the envelope full of evidence toward the prosecutor. The prosecutor frowned as he picked up the manila folder and began pouring its contents on the desk.

Chapter 19

Ed was anxious to be released. He wanted to find out if Jason had any new clues about Leslie's disappearance. He smiled when he saw Jason in the waiting room after he was discharged.

"What've you found out?" Ed asked as soon as he was in Jason's car. Jason smiled, knowing Ed couldn't wait another second.

"I haven't found out much to be honest. But you'll be happy to know that I have a present for you. A man by the name of Chris is waiting at your residence for questioning. I'm convinced he knows more than he's saying, but we'll have to get it out of him." Jason said, barely keeping the speedometer on the legal speed limit.

"How did you manage that?" Ed asked barely able to contain his excitement.

"I have lots of good street friends who owe me favors and didn't mind escorting him to your place and holding him there until we arrived," Jason laughed.

Ed wasted no time jumping out of the car when Jason pulled into his driveway.

"Wait! Dammit!" Jason cussed as Ed ran through the front door of his home.

"Where is he!" Ed exclaimed, frantically looking around for Chris. He found Chris in his den, held at gun point by two thuggish looking men. When Ed set eyes on Chris he practically tripped over his own two feet trying to get to him. Jason ran over to Ed and latched onto his arm to keep him from killing Chris before they got any information out of him. Ed shook Jason off and plowed a doubled fist into Chris' face. Ed experienced a few moments of joy when Chris's head snapped back, blood spilling out of his mouth and onto the floor.

"Where is she you Son-Of-A-Bitch!" Ed snarled, ready to punch Chris again, when Jason stepped in.

"Ed calm down!" Jason yelled as he pulled Ed away from Chris. Chris used the back of his hand to wipe the blood from his mouth.

"I don't know where she is. She was at the hotel in Vegas when I left for the airport," Chris mumbled.

"I don't believe you, you sick Son of a Bitch! I don't believe you! Why would Leslie stay in Vegas alone and allow you fly back to Atlanta without her?"

"She said she didn't want to come back to Atlanta and that she needed time to think. She knew I was coming back at the end of the week, so she decided to stay," Chris yelled.

"If I find out that you had anything to do with her disappearance you will be a dead man!!!" Ed screamed as he tried to break free from Jason's hold and lunge toward him again.

"I refuse to stand here and be assaulted and accused of something so serious. I love Leslie. I would never do anything to hurt her. I demand to be released!" Chris yelled. Something in Ed's gut didn't believe Chris's story but he knew there was no way to prove it without evidence.

"What do you want us to do with him?" One of the guys asked, their guns still drawn.

"Kill him!" Ed yelled.

“No, we can’t kill him. We might need him later,” Jason replied. He turned to his friends. Take this piece of shit out of here but give him a little taste of what will happened if he tells anyone about this meeting. Then drop his sorry ass off at home.” Jason said to his friend.

“You two won’t get away with this!” Chris screamed as the two guys dragged him out of the room.

“I know he’s lying! We should’ve killed him!” Ed yelled.

“You just got out of jail, you ready to go back already? Listen, I have to go take care of some business, I’ll touch bases with you later,” Jason said before walking out the door. Ed walked to his bar and poured himself a drink before plopping down on a chair and pulling out his cell phone. He dialed Mia’s number.

"Hello?" Mia answered.

"Mia it's me Ed. They released me from jail today. They found evidence that I wasn't the one who killed Tammy and dropped all the charges against me. Can you come over? I need you tonight."

"Yes, baby, what time?" Mia asked barely able to contain her excitement.

"In about an hour." Ed said as he took a drink.

"Okay, see you in about an hour." As soon as they hung up Mia started dancing around the room. Her man was out of jail! She didn't stop to wonder what evidence they found that was strong enough for the prosecutor to drop the charges against him. All she could think about was that with Leslie out of the way, she finally had the man she loved all to herself. Mia stopped dancing long enough to bend down and pick up her Chihuahua, hugging him and giving him a quick kiss on the head before placing him back on the floor and singing and dancing her way into the bathroom.

Mia raced from her car to the door of Ed's beautiful home and couldn't contain her excitement when Ed opened the door.

"Hi!" Mia squeaked as she jumped into Ed's arms. Ed squeezed her butt cheeks, taking a moment to appreciate the lushness of her ass. He could already feel himself getting hard and was reluctant to let her go.

"You smell amazing and you feel so much better than amazing!" Ed said as he escorted Mia toward his bar. He made them both cocktails. A salty margarita on the rocks for her, and a scotch straight up for him. Ed downed his drink before walking over to Mia and pulling her into his arms. Mia felt like she was melting with each nearly bone crushing kiss. His avid tongue sought out the depths of her mouth and his cock throbbed with the need to feel that warm, wet tongue against his skin. Mia moaned as her quick hands roamed over Ed's hard body. She still couldn't believe that she was with Ed. She hadn't really wanted anything bad to happen to Leslie, but she certainly wasn't going to complain about the circumstances at the moment. As Ed ravaged Mia's mouth, his hands worked her skirt up past her hips. He was pleasantly surprised that she was naked beneath the skin-tight leather. Not able to hold off any more, he unzipped his jeans to expose his hard shaft. Mia's mouth watered with a hunger to taste him. She positioned herself in between Ed's legs and got down on her knees. She didn't waste any time putting his large throbbing manhood into her mouth. Ed moaned as Mia began sucking on his dick like it was a cherry lollipop. She took her time, allowing her tongue to explore every inch of him.

"Oh, my goodness, how I've missed you baby." Ed moaned as Mia continued to massage his dick with her wet mouth and tongue. After Mia was satisfied that Ed was on the verge of explosion, she released him. She took a condom out of her purse and tore the wrapper off before sliding it down his big juicy manhood. Mia decided that tonight, she wanted to be the one to make love to Ed, she wanted Ed to be her sexual prisoner. Mia pulled a pair of nylon stockings out of her purse. She took Ed by the hand and led him to one of the guest rooms. After closing the door, she pushed Ed on the bed and tied his hands above his head. Then she mounted him. She began moving her hips up, down, and around as she placed kisses all over his face, down to his ear. She stopped long enough to nibble on his earlobe before continuing her journey of kisses down his neck to his nipples. She took her time sucking on each masculine nipple as she continued to move her hips. Expertly moving his manhood deeply in and out of her womanhood.

"How does it feel baby?" Mia whispered in heated passion.

"Oh, my goodness, it feels so good baby, so good. You're so wet." He exclaimed.

"Did you miss it baby, do you love it?" Mia asked as she began moving her hips faster.

"Oh yes baby, I missed it!" Ed yelled.

"Tell me this is your pussy," Mia whispered."

"This is my pussy!" Ed yelled. Mia began pouncing up and down even faster. Sweat began rolling down her back as she continued to move back and forth, up and down. She could feel her own excitement building. As her body gave way to orgasmic pleasure, Mia began screaming.

"Oh Ed, I love you, I love you so much! I'm about to cum baby!" She screamed. Ed smiled as he felt her body tense up as her womanhood tightened up around his dick.

"Untie me, it's my turn," Ed whispered. Mia did as she was told, releasing the knot from the stocking and freeing his hands. Ed picked Mia up, straddling her legs around his waist. He sat down in a chair next to the bed with Mia's legs still straddled around his waist. He began bouncing her body up and down on his lap as he moved his hard dick in and out. Just when Mia thought she couldn't take any more. Ed stood up and placed

Mia on the ground, turning her around and bending her over the chair. As he entered her womanhood from behind, he moved his hips fast, going deep and beating her pussy. Mia screamed out with both pain and pleasure.

"Leslie!" Ed screamed out in passion as his body finally found orgasmic release. Mia's head quickly bounced up, a frown creased her forehead as color drained from her face.

"Did you just call me Leslie!" Mia screamed.

Chapter 20

"Come on girl, you need to get up, we need to continue travelling. If we're lucky we should finally arrive today just after sunset," the old lady snapped as one of the guards yanked Leslie out of the bed. After getting dressed and being forced to eat some type of weird bread and milk mixture, Leslie was blindfolded and placed in the back of a van. Just as the old Lady had warned, they seemed to travel for hours, only stopping to refuel.

Finally, the van stopped again. Leslie heard the door to the van open and then strong hands pulled her out of the van and turned her around, removing the blindfold from her eyes. She blinked several times as her eyes adjusted to the bright rays of sunlight. What Leslie saw next surprised her. Before her was a large golden gate with two soldiers standing on each side holding rifles. Beyond the gate appeared to be a large castle. Leslie was pushed forward and led through the gates. She was placed into a horse driven wagon.

Leslie's body rocked back and forth against the wagon as it made its way down the rocky road toward the castle. Leslie couldn't help but be amazed at the beautiful scenery and all the people lined up on both sides of the road.

As the wagon made its way toward the castle Leslie began to hear the people cheering. Once the wagon finally stopped, Leslie was pulled from the wagon and escorted into the castle. She was led down a long corridor to a huge set of French double doors that were intricately carved in some sort of Latin script. Leslie bit her lip trying to remember anything from her college courses on Latin, but the fog of exhaustion weighed heavy on her mind. She was none too gently pushed through the doors when they slowly opened.

"Hello Princess," a tall lanky guard said, offering his arm. Leslie wasn't feeling cooperative but after a stern and almost deadly look from the guard, she took his arm. He led her down another eerie, barely lit corridor permeated with the smell of coconuts and palm trees. Leslie thought it was a little overdone and couldn't wait to tell this Abacus person exactly what was on her mind. She was led into a dark room with what seemed to be hundreds of lit candles. Red, purple, and green candles were all over the room. A magnificent bed was ornately decorated with satin sheets, and Leslie could just imagine what this Abacus had dreamed up in his perverted head about what he planned to do with her. She would have laughed if she wasn't feeling such a strong mixture of petrified and pissed off.

"Well hello beautiful!" A deep voice called from the darkness. Leslie turned toward the sound.

"You look stunning Leslie," the heavily accented voice said from the shadows. Much to her chagrin, Leslie liked being called stunning. Her voice wavered with nerves and anger as she replied.

"You Son-Of-A-Bitch! Get out here and face me like a man!" Leslie watched a dark shadow step out, his identity still concealed by the darkness. Leslie all but fainted, she was finally coming face to face with the man who had ordered her kidnapping. She stumbled onto the bed and let out a half moan of agony as she tried to crawl across the slippery sheets.

"Are you truly that afraid of me Leslie?" The shadow asked. Leslie couldn't answer, and only shook her head, 'no' in an attempt to seem brave.

"I'm not here to hurt you Leslie.

"What..what," Leslie stuttered "What're you going to do with me?"

"There's no need to be afraid Leslie, I would never hurt you." The most handsome man she had ever seen in her life stepped out of the shadows and approached her with the stride of a stallion. Something about him looked familiar. Leslie knew she had seen him before but couldn't remember where.

"I'm glad you made it to me safely my love. I've been waiting for you." He said with a deep accent as he took Leslie's hand and kissed it.

"Who, who are you and why have you brought me here?" Leslie stuttered. She couldn't get over his beauty or how familiar he looked. She felt a spark deep inside her being.

"My name is Prince Abacus. I've brought you to Arabia to be my wife. Don't you remember me? You're still just as beautiful as you were in college. I've loved you for a very long time Leslie." Suddenly it clicked, and Leslie realized where she recognized from.

"Wait a minute, you're Abe from my World History Class in college, right?" She asked.

“You are correct, my love,” Abacus answered confidently.

“I never knew your real name was Abacus. You never told me you were a prince. I thought you were just a foreign exchange student?” Leslie stated as she stared into his eyes. He had aged a lot since college but was still very handsome in a rugged type of way.

“I didn’t tell anyone because I didn’t want to be treated like a prince. I wanted to be treated like a normal person for once in my life. I came to America to study. If everyone there knew who I was, they would have treated me like as a prince instead of a normal college student,” he replied. Then came the question that haunted every fiber of her being.

“Why did you have me kidnapped?” She asked forcefully. As soon as the words came out of her mouth she had a sense of dread.

“I didn’t. I found you by accident. I was in Russia on political business when a colleague took me with him to an underground sex slave auction. You appeared to be heavily sedated but even in slumber I recognized you immediately. When I saw you, I knew I had to save you. I also knew this was my opportunity to make you mine. I’ve always loved you Leslie," Abacus stated. Leslie was shocked. She didn't know what to say. Abacus walked over to her and took hold of her hand.

"You will become my wife." He said grinning from ear to ear.

"I'm already married." Leslie replied. She felt a tingle run through her body when Abacus touched her.

"Your marriage in America, holds no legality in Arabia. You might as well forget your old life because you won't be returning!" Abacus immediately regretted his harsh words when he saw the hurt and pain in her eyes. He cupped her face in his hands.

"I haven't seen any other woman in my dreams but you since the first day I laid eyes on you. I love you Leslie and I very much want you to be mine."

Leslie's head swam with every emotion imaginable. She knew this had to be some crazy dream. She prayed someone was looking for her. Where was Chris? Why hadn't he been there to save her? Leslie asked herself as she stared into the eyes of the man who was about to become her Arabian husband.

Chapter 21

Jason and Ed sat in front of the television watching the surveillance video from the hotel. Ed felt his heart swell with pain as he watched the two men dressed as housekeepers pushing the large linen crate out of Leslie's hotel room.

"So, have you gotten anything back on the fingerprints you submitted?" Ed asked as he turned away from the television.

"No not yet. The police work too slow. I think it would be better if we caught a plane to Vegas and searched for the men ourselves."

"Um, isn't that kind of dangerous?" Ed asked with a concerned look on his face.

"What are you scared? By the time the police go into action, Leslie could be dead. I think we need to go and get as much information from the streets as we can on our own," Jason said as he continued to watch the video.

“But how are we going to find them?”

“I have connections in Las Vegas. Don’t worry, we’ll find them.” Jason replied as he began rewinding the tape. Ed turned back toward the television just in time to see Chris walking down the hotel hallway with one of the guys who had kidnapped Leslie. Ed jumped up from the couch.

"Did you just see that?" Ed yelled as he grabbed the remote from Jason and pushed rewind.

"Wow, that's Chris with the same guy that pushed the linen cart out of Leslie's room and from the time stamp, it looks like it was just two days earlier." Jason exclaimed as he closely examined the video.

"I knew that Motherfucker had something to do with her disappearance. We need to give this motherfucker a visit and get more information out of him." Ed yelled with rage.

"I agree," Jason said as he walked into his bedroom and came back out putting the safety on his 9mm. He put the gun in the waistband of his pants before glancing at his watch.

"The dude is probably still at work. Let’s pay him a visit and shake some information out of him." Jason said as he grabbed his jacket and car keys. Ed jumped up from the couch, turned off the television, and followed Jason out the front door.

An hour later, Ed and Jason pulled into the parking garage of the East Estates Professional Building. After finding a parking spot Jason turned toward Ed before getting out of the car.

"Okay listen, we're only going to rough him up a little. Remember that you just got released from prison. I don't want you going back for really killing someone," Jason stressed with a serious look on his face.

"Don't worry, I'm not going to do anything I'm going to regret," Ed said before getting out the car. The men walked toward the entrance of the building and got on the elevator. Jason and Ed were silent as they rode the elevator up to the first floor. They stepped off the elevator into the lobby and walked up to the front desk.

"Hello, what floor is Anderson & Peterson Corporation located?" Jason asked.

"Do you have an appointment? I have to call upstairs to confirm your arrival for your appointment," the receptionist stated.

"Ah, no, we were referred to this company by a friend," Ed replied quickly.

"I'm sorry but you'll need to make an appointment before I can allow you to go upstairs, its company policy." The petite receptionist stated in a professional voice.

"Well could you at least call upstairs and see if Mr. Chris Peterson is in today?" Jason asked.

"Sure, just one moment please." The receptionist said as she dialed the number.

"Hello, is Mr. Peterson in today? He has two potential clients who would like to schedule an appointment." She said into the phone as she smiled at Ed and Jason.

"Oh, he's gone? Oh, okay, I'll let them know," she said before hanging up the phone. "I'm sorry but Mr. Peterson has gone out of the country on business and won't be back for a few weeks. Let me give you the number so that you can schedule an appointment with his secretary," she stated as she wrote the information down on a business card.

"Thanks," Jason said smiling as he took the card. Both men got on the elevator with an irritated look on their faces.

"So, he went on vacation, how convenient. Look since we have no idea where he went, I think we should take a trip to Vegas and find those two guys," Jason said as he stopped next to his car and pulled his car keys out of his pocket.

"I know someone who knows exactly where he's at." Ed said as he pulled out his cellphone and dialed Mia's number. Ed was even more irritated when her answering machine came on.

"Mia call me as soon as you get this message, I need to see you tonight." Ed said before abruptly ending the call. Ed had to admit that he was surprised to get her voicemail, she usually answered the phone no matter what time he called. Ed hoped she wasn’t still upset with him for accidently calling her Leslie's name during sex.

"I'm not leaving Atlanta until I find him," Ed yelled as they got in the car.

Chapter 22

Mia's body shook uncontrollably as her core body temperature continued to fall. Her hands and feet were numb, and she couldn't control the tears that coursed down her face. She closed her eyes tight against the pain and prayed that someone would find her.

The freezer door opened and Chris along with two other men entered the room. Chris walked in limping. One of his arms were in a sling.

"You couldn't just leave shit alone could you?" Chris said, his voice a mixture of anger, regret, and frustration, "Did you think I'd never find out that you paid to have Ed protected while he was jail? Ed should've never made it out of jail alive! He should be dead! But because of your interference he's still alive! Do you realize what I've gone through, how far I've come just to get to this point? I've spent ten years planning this out. I won't rest until I know Ed's paid with his life for what he did to my sister!" The venomous hatred that came out of Chris scared Mia to the core.

She'd always known he was easy to piss off, but this was going a little overboard. Still Mia sat as still as she could, and never said a word for fear she'd anger him more. Mia wanted to ask what happened to him and who had beat him up. From the look of his bruises, it looked like someone had wanted to teach him a serious lesson. But she knew better than to ask.

"Ed and his men paid me a visit Mia! You see what they did to me? None of this would've happened if you hadn't interfered!" Chris yelled as if he had read her mind.

"I'm so pissed! I should make you pay for your betrayal with your life but I'm not ready to end your life yet." Chris said, and just when Mia was about to relax, she felt Chris' massive hand lifting her off the floor by her throat.

"But I swear, if you ever betray me again, I'll snap this pretty little neck of yours like a twig, do you understand?" Mia's tears continued as she barely shook her head, "yes."

Chris dropped her onto the hard floor and signaled two of his goons to help her up. They carried her out of the freezer and took her to a room where a nurse began tending to her frostbitten hands and feet. Several hours later, her core temperature was finally back to normal, but the extensive damage to her fingers was almost beyond repair. The nurse chastised Chris for leaving her in the freezer for so long.

"It's one thing to discipline her, and another to completely torture her. If I can save her fingers, you'll owe me dearly." Chris shrugged off the chagrin he felt and moved on to the next phase of his plan. Mia would fall in line, or she'd have to pay the consequences.

The damage to the fingers on Mia's left hand had been severe. Once the nurse realized that Mia needed a doctor, she called Dr. Marshall. He admitted her into the hospital and performed corrective surgery on her hand. After ten hours of surgery, the doctor was only able to save three of the fingers on her left hand. Her thumb and index finger had to be amputated.

Mia cried as she looked at her bloody bandaged hand. It was at that moment that Mia decided that no longer would she be Chris's puppet. For years she had been Chris's right-hand person, doing all the dirty work for his schemes. When Chris first told her about the plan to get revenge on the man who was indirectly responsible for his sister and his mother's death, she had felt a sense of loyalty to Chris and told him she would do whatever needed to be done. Mia never expected to fall in love with Ed. She still couldn't figure out how Chris had found out that she had Ed protected while he was in jail.

Mia had been caught off guard when she returned home from Ed's house and found Chris's men waiting on her. She had been so deep in thought, upset with Ed for yelling out Leslie's name during sex, that she didn't see them when they walked up behind her while she was unlocking her front door. They covered her mouth and nose with a cloth that had a foul smell that was so strong, it knocked her unconscious. When she finally regained consciousness, she was locked in a freezer.

"You're going to pay for what you've done to me Chris, and you're going to pay big," Mia sobbed uncontrollably.

Mia was about to go to bed when the doorbell rang. Her heart suddenly leaped for joy hoping that it was Ed. But the happiness was short lived when she opened the door and saw Chris standing in the doorway.

"Well, I'm glad to see you're out of the hospital," Chris said as he walked past her and into the house without bothering to wait for an invitation.

"What do you want Chris?" Mia demanded.

"Well now, is that any way to greet the love of your life? I know you're not still upset," he chuckled.

"Upset! Why should I be upset with the man who locked me in a freezer and caused my fingers to be amputated? Look I'm not sure what you want, but please say whatever it is and then leave. I am through being your puppet Chris, it's over between us!" Mia yelled. Chris walked over to her and grabbed her by the neck. Mia grimaced from the pain.

"It's over when I say it's over!" He said before forcefully kissing her lips.

Mia struggled against the kiss as much as the pain, but Chris was stronger by far. Mia could feel her head swimming and fought for air. Chris didn't let go and the ever-increasing pressure was turning her world black. She whimpered out a plea, but it fell on deaf ears.

Chris watched Mia's eyes widen and felt a pang of deep arousal. She was a gorgeous woman, even with her mangled hand. He ripped her clothes and ran rough hands over her body. Squeezing her breasts until pain etched itself across her features. When she bucked and struggled against him, Chris slapped her across the face so hard that her head snapped to the side. She knew it was useless to continue to fight him.

"I say when it's over Mia!" Chris said, anger and arousal now a keen mixture in his blood. Mia was silent, she had already retreated inside herself to help her survive the rape.

Chris, past the point of no return in his own mind, he plunged into her core, deep and ruthless. Over and over again, he tore from her the only sense of dignity she'd ever had. He finished with her quickly and then stood up to dress. And even when Mia curled into a small ball on the floor, Chris didn't feel for her.

“I’m going to Vegas for a little while, I’ll be staying at the Mirage Resort. Hold down the office while I’m gone baby and call me if you need me before I get back.” Chris said as if he hadn’t just raped her. He chuckled as he walked out of her apartment. Mia laid on the floor and cried for hours before she finally was able to pull herself together.

"You'll pay for this Chris!" Mia screamed. She knew it was no point in going to the police. She picked up the phone and dialed Ed's number. She waited as the voice mail came on.

"Ed call me when you get this message. Chris is on his way to Las Vegas. He'll probably be staying at the Mirage Resort. He knows where Leslie is." She said before ending the call.

Chris tossed his suitcase onto the hotel bed and started unpacking. He was glad to be back in Vegas. After getting worked over by Ed and his goons, Chris felt it was best to stay away from Atlanta until things cooled off. His thoughts went to Mia. He'd never admit to anyone that he felt bad about her injuries. But he knew she'd recover and eventually realize how important it was to stay loyal to him. After all, he was the one who saved her from that pimp and gave her a new life. If it wasn't for him, she'd still be a strung-out prostitute. He smiled when he thought about how magnificent a fuck she was. His dick grew hard when he thought about her. The thought of how she used to suck him made him grow hard. He decided to postpone unpacking, he showered, dressed for success, and picked up his cherry red, convertible from the Valet an hour later. Hitting the strip had never been hard for him. Even before he'd met Mia, he'd been well versed in the ways of finding the best prostitute for the job.

It didn't take Chris long to find the "hooker hangout." He cruised up and down the strip a few times before finding a feisty looking redhead who has his cock throbbing before he even stopped the car. Her cherry red lip gloss accentuated full lips. Her low-cut top gave him just enough show of her ample breasts to have him aching, and her tight booty shorts revealed a big ass and legs that never ended.

Chris honked the horn, pointed and smiled when she approached his car.

"What'll it be sugar?" She asked in a sultry voice. Chris laid out the details, paid half upfront and took her for a ride. They reached his favorite spot in ten minutes flat, driving well over the posted speed. Chris had hardly put the car in park when "Cherry" began the whole process for which she'd been nicely compensated. Chris watched as Cherry quickly maneuvered between him and the steering wheel. Her hands were magnificent, and he almost couldn't wait to feel what her mouth could do. She expertly sheathed him in a non-lubricated lamb-skin condom and before long Chris was lost in the sensations of her wonderful mouth. He smiled as he closed his eyes and imagined she was Mia.

Cherry couldn't say that her current client was the biggest she'd ever given head to, but nonetheless, the money was worth the job. She toyed with him for several seconds before she finally let him breathe again. He was panting like a virgin trying not to come too soon. She would have smiled if she'd known him better. She lifted her short "shorts" and didn't waste time before she slid down on him. He moaned out his satisfaction and Cherry went to work.

Chris tried his best to let his mind wander like the sex therapist had told him to do. She'd been one hell of a therapist too, but nothing ever seemed to change. With an uncontrollable tensing of his body, Chris came hard after just a few short strokes of Cherry's wet center.

Cherry sat back in the passenger seat, and after a few moments Chris drove her back downtown, paid her the other half of her money, and said "goodbye." Cherry smiled, kissed his cheek and got out of the red convertible that was so much like her personality. She watched Chris drive away and hoped that she would get at least ten more "less than a minute man," before the night was over.

Ed could barely sit still in his Las Vegas hotel room as he waited for a call from Jason saying that they could finally go after that piece of shit Chris Peterson. He had to remember to return Mia's call when he returned to Atlanta. He wanted to thank her for leaving that message on his phone, tipping him with the information about Chris's whereabouts and that Chris knew where Leslie was. Thoughts crammed into each other as Ed tried to separate thoughts of Leslie from those of Mia. His heart hurt for his wife, but his body ached for Mia's touch.

What the fuck is wrong with me? I'm sitting here, worried sick about my wife while I fantasize about fucking another woman. I'm a sick son of a bitch! The thoughts continued to scramble through Ed's brain. When the hotel phone finally rang, Ed jumped up to answer it.

"It's about damn time!" Ed practically yelled into the receiver. His body almost shook with the need to act. He knew he'd never be able to sit still for long with his entire life in an uproar. He needed Leslie to help him feel normal, and he needed Mia to help him feel at all.

"Chris just returned to his hotel."

“Okay, I’ll be there to get you in a few, meet me in front of the hotel.” Ed replied before ending the call. Ed smiled as he headed out the door.

They caught Chris just before he was able to leave his hotel room again.

"Well hello Christopher," Jason said as he knocked him back into the room. Chris hadn't seen the punch coming and took it full in the face. Before he could recover, Jason punched him again, knocking the wind out of him and reopening a wound above his left eye. Jason pulled out his gun and pointed it at Chris before he had a chance to get up and throw a punch. Chris quickly raised his arms up in the air.

"Whatever you guys are looking for, I don't have it." Ed lifted Chris by his shirt collar and nailed him square in the face, not even close to satisfied when he felt, and heard Chris’s nose break. Chris spit blood out onto the carpet and tried again,

"I'm serious, I have no idea what you guys are after," Chris screamed.

"How about Leslie for starters, you sick fuck!" Ed yelled.

"Chill out Ed, let him talk," Jason yelled as he threw Chris a towel. Chris grabbed the towel, crawled over to a chair and staunched the flow of blood from his eye and nose as he stared at them through the eye that wasn't swelling shut.

"Look, I know you're sore over the fact that I fucked your wife, but when I left Vegas, she was absolutely fine," Jason let Chris dig his grave before even mentioning the video. Ed punched him in the face one more time for good measure as Chris put the hotel surveillance tape in the DVD player and pushed play.

Ed watched the color drain from Chris's face as he watched the video.

"Where's my wife?" Ed asked again, the venom of hatred so close to the surface that it practically reached out to choke Chris. Realizing that there was no longer a reason to lie, Chris started laughing.

"Don't tell me you're actually worried about her?" Chris said, not trying to conceal his sarcasm. "You don't really love her. She deserves so much better than you!" Chris squirmed from the throbbing pain in his face as he talked.

"You don't know anything about what I feel for my wife." Ed held fast to his temper and waited. He wasn't leaving until he had some solid evidence about Leslie's abduction and whereabouts.

"I know that you brought her to a swinger's party, so you could fuck other women. If you really loved her, you wouldn't have been willing to share her with strangers. You're a disgrace to men everywhere who work hard to love their wives. You'll never be faithful to Leslie. Why not give her a clean break and you'll be free to screw anything with two legs?" Jason stepped up to Chris before Ed could pummel him anymore.

"Just tell us where you sent her before I allow Ed to beat you to death or I decide to shoot you and end your pathetic life!" Jason yelled. Chris's' color turned a little ashen at the thought of being shot or punched again, he could barely see as it was, and his head hurt like a motherfucker. He mulled over his choices and decided to come clean.

"I believe they sent her to Russia. I'm not sure. I had contacts who were very interested in your wife, for less than honorable reasons. She is a tart after all. My job was to get her to Vegas, what they did with her after that I have no idea. I'm only the U.S. contact."

"Tell us their names!" This time it was Jason who was growing impatient, and when Chris smiled, he'd had enough. Jason clocked Chris so hard with the gun that he fell backward and hit his head on the floor, when he didn't move Jason checked his breathing and gave Ed a thumb up.

"I'll stay with him until I get the names of his contacts and the police arrive. You go pack and pick up two tickets to Russia. We'll find them Ed, and when we do, they'll lead us to Leslie." Jason didn't add that Chris had some good points about Ed and Leslie's relationship.

"Did you get the information?" Ed asked as he impatiently paced up and down the corridor, while he and Jason waited to board their plane. Jason smiled, and Ed knew that he'd been successful.

"Yep, One Mr. Aldus Brodey, a man named Roberto, and a brute by the name of Sheamus McMullen." Jason said he took his boarding pass from Ed. They didn't say anything else until they were in the privacy of their first-class seats.

"Where's Chris?"

"I handed him over to the Vegas police along with the hotel surveillance tape."

"I can't wait to find these Motherfuckers." Ed said, shifting in his seat as if he couldn't get comfortable. He ordered a strong scotch straight up and downed the drink in one giant gulp.

Neither one of the men mentioned what they were both thinking. There was a possibility that they'd never find Leslie alive.

Ed and Jason landed in Russia to the sound of pouring rain. They quickly made their way through the airport security and grabbed their luggage. Since Jason was familiar with driving in the foreign country, Ed didn't mind letting him get the rental car. Within an hour, they were headed toward Cork. They stopped at a small pub and grabbed something to eat and each indulged in a fresh pint of Guinness. They talked quietly about where they'd start their search.

Chapter 23

Leslie couldn't believe her eyes as Abacus laid her gently on the bed. There were jewels everywhere, beautiful hand stitched tapestries, and a huge four-poster canopy bed that took Leslie's breath away.

"All this, for me?" She asked.

"All this and more, my princess! Just say, I do!" He said before kissing her so passionately that she melted in his arms. Abacus grew hard at her response to his kisses. "Marry me, now!" He whispered as he trailed kisses down her neck.

"But I keep telling you, I'm already married," she said breathlessly.

"And I keep telling you that your marriage in the U.S. holds no merit here," He said in between kisses.

Over the last two months, Leslie had grown to love Abacus. She couldn't help herself. At first, she had tried to hate him, but he had worn her down with his constant declarations of love and affection. He had patiently waited and worked hard to gain her trust. They eventually began having long talks. He told her everything about his life and she told him everything about her life, her marriage to Ed, everything that had happened before she went to Vegas, and her affair with Chris. After a while, her walls of ice began falling and she began falling in love with her kidnapper. Everyone in the palace treated her like she was a queen. She wanted for nothing. If she even hinted at wanting or needing something, it was given to her in abundance. How could she not fall in love with a man who gave her everything?

"There's just one more thing that bothers me," she said.

"What is it, sweetheart?" Abacus asked looking worried.

"Your other wives. I've come in second place for eight years, I don't want to be someone's trophy wife again," she answered with tears in her eyes.

"Leslie, I married them out of duty. In our custom, I needed heirs. I'm marrying you because you're the only woman I've ever loved! I promise you, you're the only woman I will come to from now on," he said earnestly.

"Then what're we waiting for? Let's go get married!" Leslie replied happily.

Abacus chuckled deeply at Leslie's exuberance. She was still the same woman he'd known way back in college. She had stunned him with her beauty and earned his love with her zest for life, and her quick mind. It shamed men everywhere that her husband had treated her as less than his equal.

"Leslie, before we do this, I need you to understand that you will have responsibilities. As my wife you'll be expected to attend parties and cabinet meetings with me. I'll need your brain as well as your body to make this kingdom all it can be. Because," Abacus paused as he pulled her closer, "I love them both equally." Leslie felt tears sting her eyes. Never in a million years had she been loved so completely or wanted to give love back so entirely. Her hands shook as Abacus slipped a huge ruby-diamond ring on her finger. She felt both the weight of the ring, and the steps she was taking to change her future.

"Abe, the only thing I need to be sure of right now, is that Ed's family will never find me again. If I'm going to do this and become your wife. I want to belong to you completely. I don't want anything from my past to ever find me here with you."

Abacus reassured Leslie that she was safe with him, wanted and needed by him. He promised her that absolutely nothing or no one would ever come between them.

Leslie smiled as she was pampered and fussed over by the servants as they prepared her for her wedding. She was giddy like a schoolgirl and couldn't believe how much her life had changed in such a short time. Even though Abacus had promised her that Ed would never find her, deep in her soul she didn't believe that. She knew Ed's family would stop at nothing to rescue her and bring her back to the US. They wouldn't rest until they found her. But it didn't matter, when that time came, Leslie would let them know that she had fallen in love and was happy with her new life as Abacus's wife.

"Are you ready dear?" The little granny asked as she placed an ancient necklace around

Leslie's neck. Leslie fingered the delicate gold clasp and wondered how old it was. She looked in the mirror and studied her reflection. Her thick hair was covered with a beautiful white hijab. A veil covered her face. She smelled of honeysuckle soap and Jasmine perfume. Nothing too strong, subtle and enticing. She smiled and replied to the older woman's question.

"I don't believe Ms. Fairline, that I've ever been more ready for anything in my entire life." The old woman's wrinkled face broke out in a wide smile, and she hustled everyone along, helping Leslie with her dress. When Leslie entered the long hallway. she heard the pipe organ playing strains of beautiful Arabian music. She glanced at the old woman who simply gestured her down the elongated foyer.

Leslie looked again down the foyer and took a deep breath to calm her jittery nerves. She started slowly down the long hallway, letting her eyes adjust to everyone who sat quietly watching her. When she looked up she could finally make out Abacus waiting for her. He was stunningly handsome in a gorgeous white tux. His dark curly hair hidden with a black hijab. His smile reached his eyes and she couldn't wait to kiss that wonderful mouth. The liquid fire that shot between her legs at the mere thought of kissing him, brought a smile to her lips and made her steps a little quicker.

"You look unbelievably amazing!" Abacus said when she finally reached him. The priest performed a Catholic ceremony and before she knew it, Leslie was Princess Leslie Minestra (Minnes-trah). Abacus kissed her so deeply that even the shyest of his subjects cheered.

They thoroughly enjoyed the reception into the early morning hours before finally making their escape amid applause and raucous cheering.

"I've been waiting for this forever it seems." Abacus said, obviously excited to finally have Leslie to himself. Leslie couldn't contain her own excitement, kissing Abacus fully, passionately as he scooped her up to carry her further into his chambers. They kissed past the sitting room, past the den and study, and well past the anterior chamber. When they finally reached the bedroom their kiss only turned up the already smoldering heat that passed like waves between them.

Abacus broke the kiss for a split second to place Leslie back on her feet so that he could undress her. As soon as her feet were planted firmly on the floor he resumed kissing her while fumbling with the buttons on her dress.

"Tear it off!" Leslie whimpered as he kissed her jaw. Abacus didn't think twice, he did as she asked, grabbed a large handful of the dress and ripped it. Leslie quickly removed her slip, so she was standing in nothing but her white lace panties. She could tell he liked what he, judging by the bulge inside his pants. The thought of him wanting her sent liquid fire coursing through her body all over again, leaving a pool of hot moisture between her thighs. Leslie pulled off his tux jacket, then yanked his shirt over his head not bothering to unbutton it, and she kissed him fiercely and passionately as her hands roamed his muscled chest. Moving downward, Leslie unzipped his pants and pulled them and his boxers down around his ankles in one swift motion. She sank to her knees and took his bulging manhood into her mouth.

"Ahhhh!" He moaned. She took her time tasting and feeling every inch of him.

"Ohhhh baby, I need you NOW!" He shouted. She released his cock from her mouth and he pulled her to her feet. He picked her up to place her on the bed and she wrapped her legs around him pulling him on top of her. He yanked her panties off, his manhood immediately found her hot, wet entrance and thrusts into her hard.

"Ooohhh!" She moaned. Slowly they got into a rhythm meeting each other's every thrust with eagerness.

"Ahhhh!" Yelled Abacus as he pounded into her.

"Oh Abe, I'm going to come, baby! Come with me!" Leslie gasped.

"OHHH GOD, BABYYYY!!!" They screamed together as a rapture of hot lava erupted from their bodies.

Leslie was awakened by the sound of birds chirping outside their window. She smiled as she felt Abacus's strong arms around her waist. Leslie twisted her body in his arms so that she could face him. Abacus moved slightly in response to Leslie, adjusting her body to the new position. She smiled as she gazed into his handsome face. She couldn't believe that she was a princess and that she had agreed to become her kidnapper's wife. She had always thought Abacus was cute when they were in school. But he seemed so quiet and reserved back then, always into his school work. She never told any of her friends that she was attracted to him. Who would have guessed that he was a prince or that one day she would be his wife? Abacus must have sensed that she was staring at him because he suddenly opened his eyes and smiled.

"Good morning princess." He said as he kissed her on the lips.

"Good morning prince," she replied.

"It feels so good to have you in my arms, in my life, and in my bed."

"Are you alright? Is something bothering you?" He asked frowning when he noticed the sad look in her eyes.

"No, I'm just wondering what I'll do if Ed's family ever finds me. I mean I am still his wife in the eyes of America," Leslie said frowning.

"There's no need to worry about that. I'll get in touch with a lawyer friend of mine in the US and have him draw up divorce papers. All you'll need to do is sign them and then we'll have them sent to him in prison." Abacus said as he regretfully pulled away from Leslie and got out of bed.

"Is it possible that I can have more of the liquid diamonds between your lovely thighs?" He asked as he leaned over and kissed her on her forehead.

"Yes, you can have whatever you want," Leslie giggled.

"I'll be right back." Abacus said as he walked into the bathroom. Leslie sat up in the bed and laid against the large fluffy pillows as she admired her new wedding ring. The ring that Ed had given her looked like something out of a bubblegum machine compared to the rock on her finger. She wondered how Abacus's other wives would behave once they realized that Abacus wasn't going to be sleeping with them anymore. When Abacus came out of the bathroom he leaped back into the bed and pulled Leslie toward him.

Chapter 24

After searching restlessly for the last two months, Jason and Ed had finally been able to track Aldus Brodey to a small farm town outside of Dublin but wasn't sure if he was still there. The other two men were like ghosts, there wasn't so much as a speck of paper with their names on it. If Their names were actually Shaemus McMullen and Roberto anyways.

After finishing their food, they headed for their hotel and Jason started his search on foot. After warning Ed not to go traipsing off without him, Jason headed out. Ed of course thought Jason was full of himself and headed down to the pub around the corner to enjoy another pint. He entered the smoky pub just in time for the nightly music and sat down at the bar.

"What'll it be Mack?" the barkeeper asked, wiping the bar down as he came close to Ed. Ed ordered a pint of Guinness and turned to see the band. He enjoyed a few pints and finally got up to leave and head back to his room. As he turned the corner, a massive set of hands reached out and quickly slammed him against the wall of the pub.

"I hear you're looking for me Mr. Johnson. If that's the case, then I'm happy to say that ye found me!" Shaemus said as he grabbed the scruff of Ed's shirt and punched him square in the face. The last thing Ed remembered was the sound of his nose breaking before the black overwhelmed him.

By the time Jason realized that Ed had been abducted he was steaming mad. Pissed off didn't even begin to cover it. He'd finally traced Ed's motions to the pub and just outside the bar had found Ed's broken glasses. Now he'd have to use considerable resources just to find the idiot. He was beginning to wonder how they'd become friends. As soon as the thought hit he rejected it, Ed might be a piece of shit husband, and a philanderer, but he'd saved Jason's ass more than once. So, Jason tucked Ed's glasses into his blazer and went to work. The sooner he found Ed, the better.

Chapter 25

Ed woke to the pain first. God in Heaven his face hurt. He quietly took stock of his injuries, already knowing that his nose was broken. His jaw felt like someone had belted him a time or two for good measure, but Ed was pretty sure it was still intact. He didn't seem to hurt anywhere else, and as he slowly opened his eyes he realized that his predicament had gone from bad, to worse. If he wasn't mistaken, he was in a cell of some sort.

"Well good morning Mr. Johnson," Sheamus McMullen said when he entered the room. Ed looked up from his cot at the massive brute of a man. Ed wasn't a slouch and stayed in great shape for his age and physique but holy hell this man rivaled Andre the Giant.

"You broke my nose." Ed said, not ashamed that his eyes wanted to tear up at the memory. Sheamus simply smiled.

"That I did sonny, and I'll be breaking more than that here shortly if you don't give it to me straight." Ed would have sneered at the man if his face didn't feel like it'd recently gone through a meat grinder.

"I needed to find you, Roberto, and Aldus Brodey so that I could find out where you took my wife." Ed said, deciding that if he was going to die, he'd go out on honesty is the best policy He had some futile hope that they'd have pity on him and fess up.

"Sorry sonny, don't know anything about no wife. I deal in precious cargo for sure but ain't seen no Miss around these parts," Sheamus said.

"You're sure? Leslie Johnson. She's um, she's about 5'7" weighs around 145. She's smart, mouthy, and incredibly sexy. She's got thick dark hair and a tiny scar on her cheek. Freckles too. I saw you and Aldus on the hotel surveillance tape when you kidnapped her from her hotel room in Las Vegas, Nevada." Ed didn't question the tears that came to his eyes. He knew he loved Leslie, and he also knew that he was probably too late to really show her just how much she meant to him.

"Oh, that was your wife? Sheamus chuckled before he turned around and left the room. Ed sank back down on his cot to simply wait, and that wait nearly killed him.

After asking a lot of questions around town and dishing out a lot of money with the help of money wired to him by Ed's father, Jason was able to find out Ed's location. Jason decided it was time to involve the police.

The Swat team surrounded the old abandoned prison where Ed was being held captive.

"We have you surrounded, come out with your hands up!" The Sergeant yelled through the police bull horn.

After hours of negotiation, and a quick gun battle between the police and Ed's kidnappers. Ed was now a free man. Ed could not have been happier to see his best friend.

"The next time I tell you to stay put, you had better listen!" Jason yelled.

" Were you able to find out anything?" Ed asked.

"Yes, it appears that Leslie has been taken to Saudi Arabia."

"What!" Ed yelled in disbelief?"

"Yep, but I have more news that's even more disturbing. Your father informed me that your wife filed for a divorce. She's in Saudi Arabia." Jason watched as all color drained from Ed's face.

“Are you sure she's in Saudi Arabia?” Ed asked.

“Yes,” said Jason confidently.

“How can you be so sure?” Ed asked skeptically.

“The divorce papers,” he said plainly. A look of mixed confusion and sadness covered Ed's face.

“We tracked down the lawyer that sent the divorce papers, and it took a little convincing and a lot of cash, but he finally told me that the papers were sent to him through the U.S. embassy in Saudi Arabia.” Jason explained.

“Any ideas about where to find her when we get there?” Ed yelled still determined to find his wife.

“No,” Jason answered bluntly.

“So basically, you're telling me for once in your life you have no leads?” asked said Ed bitterly.

There's nothing else we can do Ed. Leslie spoke to your father and told him that she no longer wanted to be with you and that she wasn't returning to the US," Jason said shaking his head. Ed dropped down to the ground and started crying.

"Your dad said to call off the search and return to Georgia," Jason said as he helped Ed up.

Ed continued to cry as Jason drove them back to the hotel.

The next morning, they packed their bags and booked a chartered flight, courtesy of Ed's father, back to the United States. Ed had no idea what he was doing anymore. He stared out the airplane window, his eyes were focused on the clouds, but his thoughts were focused on Leslie. Did she really want a divorce? If she'd been kidnapped and brought to Saudi Arabia against her will, how could she possibly file for a divorce? Maybe she wasn't the one who filed for a divorce maybe her kidnapper forced her to do it. Maybe she was forced by her kidnappers to say she wasn't returning to the US. What if she was locked in some type of cell like he had been? Ed had seen stories on television about women who had been kidnapped, strung out on drugs, and sold into sexual slavery. All kinds of thoughts ran through his mind. He loved Leslie, he couldn't imagine his life without her. A tear slid down his face as he imagined the horrible things Leslie was probably going through at the hands of her kidnappers. What hurt him most was that he wasn't there to protect her.

After a long grueling plane ride, the plane finally landed.

"Welcome to Atlanta, you may now turn on your electronic devices." The Stewardess announced once the plane had pulled up to the gate.

"I'm glad that's over, I hate riding in planes." Jason said as he stood up to pull his carry-on luggage out of the storage compartment.

"I know me too," Ed agreed as Jason handed him his luggage. Ed pulled out his cellphone and turned it on. Once powered up, the voice mail indicator popped up. Ed dialed his voice mail and listened to ten messages from Mia. With so much going on, he had almost forgotten to call her. He quickly dialed her number as he and Jason waited to enter the aisle and exit the plane.

"Hello?" Mia answered the phone.

"Hey Mia, I got your messages, what's wrong, why were you crying?" Ed asked with a concerned look on his face. Jason overheard the urgency in Ed's voice and turned around, waiting to hear what was wrong with Mia.

" It's about Chris... I didn't tell you this before but," Mia stumbled and stuttered. "Chris had me kidnapped and raped me before he left Atlanta," she cried.

Ed's face turned pale as anger coursed through him. It wasn't enough that he was worried sick over Leslie, now he had Mia to deal with.

"Listen Mia, I'm so sorry that happened to you. But you can relax, Chris is in jail. We turned him in to the Vegas police before we left the country. You should go down to the police department and press charges against him." He said as he tried his best to console her.

"Did you find Leslie?" She asked.

"Yes and No. We know that she's in Saudi Arabia, but according to my father, she filed for a divorce and doesn't want to come back to America."

"Ed, Chris is the one who had Leslie kidnapped. He was angry because he believed that you were responsible for his sister committing suicide and his mother's death. He's been planning his revenge against you for years. Chris is so cruel. Because of him I had to have my fingers amputated!" She said as she started crying."

"Why didn't you tell me this sooner? Were you part of his scheme Mia?" Ed asked. Things were finally starting to make sense.

"I didn't have a choice Ed. He told me that if I didn't cooperate he'd kill me," Mia sobbed.

"Listen Mia, you need to go to the police and tell them everything you know, if you cooperate, maybe they'll be leant with you. But as for you and me, it's over! From this day forward, I want nothing else to do with you. You and your boyfriend destroyed my life!" Ed screamed before ending the call. Everyone on the plane was staring at Ed. Jason shook his head and patted Ed on the back before getting off the plane.

Ed felt sick. He knew that everything that had happened was all his fault. If he had never taken Leslie to Tigers that night, none of this would have happened. Because of his sexual addiction, he had loss the only woman he ever truly loved. Feeling defeated, Ed followed Jason off the plane and began walking toward the baggage claim with slumped shoulders.

Chapter 26

Leslie looked out the window in her antechamber and smiled. She couldn't remember being happier in her entire life. She was a princess! Not that it mattered much, but holy shit! She was married to the sexiest man who ever existed, and to top it all off the man was a stallion in bed. She chuckled and stood to dress. When her head started to swim, she quickly sat down and clutched her stomach. She couldn't remember feeling poorly, but now she was queasy. She waited for the feeling to pass and it soon did. She dressed and went out to find Abacus. She wandered the grounds of the small palace, astonished that in less than eight months her whole world had spun a 180*. She was divorced from Ed, become a princess, married to a prince who was crazy about her, living in a castle, and if she wasn't mistaken, she was almost positive that she was pregnant. The thought amazed her, she couldn't hide the smile that played on her lips.

She found Abacus in the paddock with the horses and couldn't wait to tell him the good news. She stepped up to the tall black stallion, Atticus, when she heard Abacus behind her.

"Now there's a sight for sore eyes," Abacus kissed the back of Leslie's neck and gave her a hug while she rubbed the power horse's neck.

"Hello, my love," Leslie whispered as she turned toward her husband.

"I have something to tell you," Leslie and Abacus said at the same time, eliciting a chuckle from them both.

"You go first," Abacus said, gesturing toward her. Leslie took a deep breath. Suddenly, she was nervous. What if Abacus didn't want children? For all the wives he had, he didn't seem to have any kids to show for it.

"I," Leslie stalled, "I was wondering if I could possibly trouble you to take a quiet lunch with me this afternoon," Abacus watched her closely for a moment, sensing that she was hiding something.

"Absolutely my darling," Abacus said. He went on to tell her that he'd gotten her a present and proceeded to show her a chestnut colored mare who was the most exquisite horse Leslie had ever seen. She squealed and immediately showered affection on the new horse. Abacus smiled, and they agreed to meet in the promenade for lunch.

Leslie walked down to the promenade a few hours later with her picnic basket in hand, and her mind full of nervous anticipation. "What if he doesn't want kids? I mean, he has all those other wives and not an heir in sight. Or worse, what if he does want kids and I miscarry again?" she said to herself.

"What was that, your highness?" Abacus asked as he came up behind her and kissed her neck.

"Nothing, Abe, just thinking out loud," she replied nervously hoping he hadn't overheard her. Her nervousness didn't escape his watchful gaze, but he knew Leslie well enough to know that she would tell him whatever was bothering her in her own time, so he swooped her up for another passionate kiss. After about five minutes of prolonged kissing, he set her down to enjoy their lunch together. Abacus opened the basket to see what was prepared, lamb and rice, his favorite! Suddenly, Leslie looked like she was going to be sick.

"Sweetheart, are you alright?" Abacus asked with a worried look. In that instant she vomited all over him.

"I'm so sorry!" She said when the vomiting finally subsided a few moments later.

"No need to apologize, baby. Let's get you back to the palace to lie down." He said lovingly as he carried her back to the palace. As soon as he placed her safely in their bed he called for his servant to bring him a clean set of clothes and help him dress her.

"Wait, there's something I need to tell you." Leslie said.

"What is it, baby?" He asked.

"Abe, I'm pregnant!" she said nervously. He froze, and slowly a smile spread across his face.

'I already know," Abacus said as he kissed her on the cheek. A surprised look covered her face.

"What do you mean you already know?" Leslie asked.

"I had a dream, and in the dream, you were pregnant. Plus, you've been throwing up a lot lately and you haven't had a cycle this month."

"Wow, I didn't realize you paid that much attention to me. So why haven't you said anything?" Abacus pulled Leslie close to him, burying his nose in her hair.

"Because I was waiting for you to confirm what I already felt," he whispered.

“Are you upset?” She asked searching his face for any evidence that he was displeased.

“How could I not be happy about such a wonderful blessing?” He asked as he kissed her deeply, wiping away all her fears.

Leslie could feel all eyes on her as she walked into the kitchen where all Abacus wives were preparing food for the evening feast. Leslie knew that Abacus's other wives were jealous of her. They made it obvious. As Leslie walked over to one of the tables and sat down to help cut potatoes. Three of his wives approached her.

"Look at her, she's so ugly!" One of the wives said with a chuckle."

"Yea, look at her ugly hair," another wife agreed. Leslie ignored them, not bothering to look up and acknowledge their presence.

"Hey ugly, I guess you think you're special." One of the wives said as she knocked the bowl of potatoes Leslie was using on the floor. Leslie jumped up from her chair.

"You three need to get away from here and leave me alone!" Leslie screamed.

"Or what, what you going to do?" One of the wives laughed.

Leslie, who even by her admission, had always been meek and easy to walk on, found new strength in the love she shared with Abacus. After years of being Ed's doormat, she realized her own power as a woman, as Abe's woman.

"I swear if you three don't leave now, I'll make you regret it for the rest of your miserable lives! And even if I can't, I'll make sure Abe can!" Leslie said, the deep timbre of her voice was all the warning the three women needed to get their asses moving. The other wives remained silent, but Leslie could see smirks and smiles appear on their faces.

"Thank you!" A little red head said, when the three women had finally disappeared. She helped Leslie pick up her potatoes before introducing herself.

"I'm Annabelle. I think I'm the youngest of Abacus' wives, so far anyways," Annabelle was admittedly stunning, with blue hazel colored eyes and a spray of freckles across her nose. She didn't look more than about eighteen. Leslie wondered if Abacus would go to Annabelle's bed once she became swollen and fat from pregnancy. She pushed the thought away quickly and offered her hand in friendship to the young girl. They chatted and laughed while they worked on their tasks for the nightly feast. Annabelle shared with Leslie things she'd learned about Abacus since they'd been married nearly two years ago now.

"You're a lucky woman Princess, although for me the Prince is rather frightening," Annabelle admitted as she watched Leslie's brow furrow and nearly laughed at her comment and concern.

"Did he hurt you?" Immediately Leslie knew she was an idiot for thinking such a thought. Abacus had never been one to show any sign of temper or frustration, and to think that he'd hurt a sweet girl like Annabelle was ludicrous.

"Oh no Princess. He, well he was very gentle with me you see. But being as he's the only man I've ever been with, it's a little bit daunting to know that he has a wealth of knowledge in an area where I have none. I was terribly embarrassed because I was so unsure of myself," Annabelle's cheeks darkened with that embarrassment now,

"Forgive me Princess, I shouldn't be sharing such intimate thoughts with you."

"Please, call me Leslie, and it's alright. I've known Abe a long time and I understand why he married. I'm not sure why there are so many wives, but I know he loves me, and in his own way he loves each of you as well." Annabelle seemed to relax. The afternoon seemed to pass quickly. When evening arrived, Leslie entered her antechamber. The mood in the room was cold and anything but relaxed.

"Please tell me that I didn't see my pregnant wife preparing supper!" Abacus said, not bothering to conceal his displeasure. Leslie nearly hid inside herself, like she would when Ed would vehemently deny his cheating, but this time she knew if she was going to be equal she had to start now.

"You did, and I'll continue to do as I please as long as I'm able!" Abacus, not wanting to let Leslie get the better of the situation played dirty.

"So, it's your pleasure to fuck me and even as a princess, to work on the meal we eat. Tell me wife, did you practice these same techniques with your other husband?" Leslie's face went ashen and Abacus instantly regretted his words. When he reached for her Leslie ran, the tears already running down her face.

Leslie skipped the evening meal and didn't return to the room she shared with Abacus until it was well past twilight. She was hurt and frustrated and so horribly confused. When she was with Ed, she took pleasure in her wifely duties. Ed had always enjoyed being pampered. He said it made him feel like a king. But Abacus was different, he didn't want her to lift a finger. Abacus treated her like a delicate flower. Leslie was starting to think that she didn't know how to handle being a princess. She tiptoed into the room and started to undress. When she was down to the last lace filigree, Abacus made his presence known.

"Never have I tolerated any wife of mine showing disrespect to me." Abacus said as he slowly caressed Leslie's shoulders. He smiled when goose bumps showed on her skin and hardened her nipples that he could see clearly through the moonlight.

"And never have I understood why men think they have to bully women to get what they want. I am used to doing housework, I am used to taking care of my man, and that includes helping to cook his meals. I enjoy it." Leslie turned in Abacus's arms and wrapped her slender ones around his waist.

"I guess we've got a lot to learn about each other huh?" Abacus said, a smirk running across his lips. When Leslie looked up her eyes were smoldering with love, and a little leftover temper. Abacus smiled fully and met her warm lips with his own. They made love slowly, as much to make up for their disagreement, as to take care of the little bundle growing in Leslie's womb. They enjoyed a cuddle afterwards and fell asleep snuggled in each other's arms.

When they woke next morning Leslie still felt a little dishearten by last night's disagreement.

"Could we talk Abe?" She asked as Abacus was getting dressed.

"Sure, baby," he replied.

"Why were you so upset about me cooking for you last night?" Leslie asked.

"Pregnant princesses don't cook," he replied simply.

"But your other wives were," she retorted. "They are not pregnant, and I don't love them like I love you. Therefore, the rule does not apply to them." he stated.

"No, it's more than that. What is it?" She asked growing frustrated.

"I don't want you to feel like you have to do things for me like you did for Ed. I have servants and other wives for that," he said honestly.

"I didn't do it because I had to. I did it because I wanted to do something nice for you to show you how much I love you," she said blinking back tears.

"Alright, you can cook for me one night a week if you wish to do so, but you must promise me that you won't over work yourself," he said.

"I promise!" Leslie said excitedly.

"Now, my dear, there's something I need to talk to you about," Abacus said as they walked toward the dining room to have breakfast together.

"Okay," she replied, nervously biting on her lower lip.

"As you know my father has become very ill recently, and he has decided that it is time to pass the crown on to me, his eldest son," he paused. "And because you're carrying my only heir, the title and position of queen rightfully goes to you," he said slowly. Leslie's mind began to swim with emotion. Finally, after a few bites of her eggs and letting it sink in she looked at Abacus and smiled.

"I don't know the first thing about running a country, how can I possibly be a good queen?" She asked.

"Your sharp mind will serve you well, my love, don't worry," Abacus chuckled.

"I'm glad you find this funny!" She said pouting.

"Listen, my love, I can abdicate the throne if it'll make you happy, but I will not take the throne without you by my side," Abacus said calmly.

"Are you crazy? I'm not going to let you give up your birthright for me!" She said with conviction.

"You will be my queen, then?" He asked smiling.

"Of course, I'll do anything to make you happy!" She said as she finished her breakfast.

"That's just what I wanted to hear," Abacus said as he leaned over and kissed her.

Chapter 27

Leslie was in the full bloom of her second trimester with all its wonderful side effects. Her other pregnancies never made it past the first trimester. She was relieved that her morning sickness had finally subsided. She still barely ate in the morning but by lunch time she was starving. Leslie managed to learn when and what to eat. She stayed away from anything fried, as the smell of grease made her ill. She craved peaches and oranges so much, that Abacus had given priority for his servants to search near and far for the ripest fruits just for her pleasure.

She walked the immense gardens daily to keep herself healthy, and at night she spent time making love to Abacus. They talked about his past, when he'd gotten married to his first wife, and why she was the first to give him an heir. She told him that she'd made a friend in Annabelle and he smiled, knowing the young woman could benefit from her wisdom.

"She's in love Abe," Leslie said one night while they cuddled after a rowdy, but cautious escapade of amazing sex. "And not with you I might add," Abacus grunted when she ran her hand up his side. He wouldn't admit to being ticklish, but she found that he would react whenever she did that.

"She's a lovely young girl, beautiful, talented, and unspoiled," Abacus said, wondering what Leslie was getting at.

"I think you should divorce her or get an annulment whichever is more appropriate. She's young and should be free to make a life with someone she loves."

“I’ll give it some serious thought.” Abacus said as he pulled her close to his body. Leslie smiled as she snuggled against her husband and drifted off to sleep.

The next morning Abacus left Leslie a note on his pillow to meet him in the promenade when she was up and feeling like it. She dressed quickly, careful with her attire to choose a dress that was regal in status but comfortable for her growing tummy.

"Hello my love," Abacus said as he placed a kiss on her forehead, "I've been thinking about our talk last night, and I've decided you're right. But not just about Annabelle. About all of my wives. I have no need for any woman but you now, so I'm annulling all my former marriages. The women will be paid a nice severance and will be free to return to their families as they choose." Leslie threw her arms around Abacus's neck and kissed him passionately. She felt his manhood harden against her skirts and stifled a moan that was all but begging to escape. She knew, even as badly as she wanted him, that mornings were not the opportune time to be intimate right now. So, she regretfully released her hold on him, placed a smoldering kiss on his lips and turned to go for her daily walk.

Leslie made weekly calls to America to talk to her family and keep her mother informed about her pregnancy. When Leslie first called Ed's father, she found out that Ed had been released from jail. She decided she wanted to speak to him. After calling and talking to her mother, Leslie dialed Ed's phone. She felt slightly nervous as the phone rang.

"Hello?" Ed answered.

“Hello Ed, it’s me Leslie.” She said softly.

“Leslie!” Ed yelled standing up.

“Yes, it’s me. I heard that you were released from jail and I wanted to check on you and see how you were doing.”

“Are you okay? Are you still in Saudi? I’ve been so worried about you.”

“Yes, I’m still in Saudi and I’m fine. You don’t need to worry about me anymore.”

“Chris and Mia are the ones who had you kidnapped and had Tammy killed. They’re both in jail awaiting a trial.”

“Wow really, well I’m glad the truth finally came out. I hope they both get life in prison.” Leslie sighed.

“Leslie please come back, please baby. I miss you so much. I’m so sorry for what I did to you, for what I did to us,” Ed sobbed.

“Ed,” Leslie began but Ed interrupted her.

“Leslie please come back to me baby!” He begged.

"Listen Ed, initially I was brought here against my will. But I met someone that I knew from college and I fell in love. He's a wonderful man and..." she paused. "We're married and I'm pregnant with twins Ed." Ed was in shock, all the color drained from his face.

"You're pregnant with twins and married?" He asked in disbelief?"

"Yes," Leslie said as she placed her hands on her swollen stomach.

"I gotta go Leslie," Ed mumbled.

"Okay, I'll call and check on you periodically," Leslie replied. She could hear the disappointment in his voice.

Unable to speak, Ed hung up on Leslie and abruptly walked away and went into the bathroom slamming the door behind him. He sat down on the toilet seat and cried like he had never cried before. For years they had been trying to have children and couldn't. Every time she got pregnant, their happiness was quickly replaced with sadness when she miscarried. To know that another man was able to experience what he couldn't made him feel like less of a man. Once his tears had subsided Ed walked out of the bathroom. He knelt next to his bed, bowed his head and began praying.

"Lord I know I've done a lot of horrible things in the past and I know I've hurt a lot of people. I deserve everything that's happened to me. Please forgive me. Please bring my wife back to me. I promise to change my ways, I promise I will never cheat again. I'll do whatever it takes, just please Lord, please bring her back to me," he cried.

Chapter 28

Leslie smiled as she walked around the nursery inspecting the room. She wanted to make sure that everything was perfect for her babies. The ultrasound showed that she was having a boy and a girl. She was too excited, a boy for Abe and a girl for her. Leslie smiled as she placed her hand over her swollen belly. She took a deep breath. The babies were due any day now. The doctor said that if she didn't go into labor on her own by next week that he was going to induce her labor. Abacus was so excited. All he talked about was how he was going to raise his son to rule the kingdom. Leslie stood up and walked over to the crib, she smiled as she picked up one of the stuffed animals. After years of wanting a child it was ironic that she would carry babies by another man full term. She figured with Ed she was always under so much stress that she couldn't carry the babies' full term. But with Abe her life was peaceful.

She called Ed a few more times over the last few months. Leslie couldn't explain why she felt the need to keep in touch with him. Ed told her that Chris was being charged with 1st degree murder in the death Tammy and her unborn child and was awaiting trial. Leslie still couldn't believe that Chris wasn't the gentle and loving man that she thought he was. The fact that he had planned to sell her into sexual slavery was still hard for her to believe. She had thought about pressing charges on him for kidnapping. But since that meant having to return to the US to testify, she had decided not to. Plus, Chris had actually done her a favor. If he hadn't had her kidnapped and sold in slavery, she never would've crossed paths with Abacus again.

She still thought a lot about Ed. Sometimes she would experience a little sadness and depression whenever she thought about all that she had allowed Ed to put her through, and then other times she worried about him. She knew that a piece of her heart would always belong to him. No matter how much she wanted to hate him, she just couldn't. There was a piece of her that would always love him. She had been feeling slight contractions throughout the day. She didn't want to alarm Abacus until she knew for sure that she was in labor.

Leslie was turning to walk to the bed when suddenly a pain tore through her midsection. This pain was much stronger than what she had been feeling. When Abacus walked into the room and saw Leslie doubled over in pain he didn't waste any time.

"Come on baby, it's time to go to the hospital." He said as he calmly guided her out of the room. Once they got into the car and began driving, Leslie's contractions suddenly began to increase and were coming one minute apart. She moaned as each contraction seemed more forceful and painful than the one before. Abacus worried that he wouldn't be able to get her to the hospital in time. They still had another fifteen miles to go. He decided to pull off the road and into a motel parking lot

"Tom, go get us a room immediately, I don't think my children are going to wait too much longer. Hurry and tell them to dial the emergency squad. Hurry!" Abacus barked at his driver. The driver jumped out the car and ran into the building.

What seemed like only two seconds later, the motel manager ran out of a building carrying keys and opened a door to one of the rooms.

Abacus had the driver pull up to the door. Abacus jumped out, pulled Leslie from the car, carried her to the room, and quickly laid her on the bed. As soon as he felt she was positioned correctly, Abacus gently pulled Leslie's skirt up and spread her legs apart. He could see what looked like the top of a curly head trying to break its way through her womanhood. Abacus quickly jumped into action.

"Hurry, bring me lots of clean towels and hot water, it looks like I am about to deliver my own babies." Abacus screamed at the manager and guards as he ran into the bathroom, tore off his shirt, and began to vigorously wash his hands and arms with soap.

Leslie turned this way and that, and finally decided that a bed wasn't going to work. The back labor was nearly unbearable in that position. Abacus thought better of telling her to stay put when she gave him a look that could kill. She quickly moved to the tub and turned the water on warm. Abacus followed with all the towels he could find, setting two thick ones under her feet. Once the tub was half way full, he helped Leslie into the tub. He watched as Leslie's face relaxed after a contraction. Her moans were low and seemed to be coming from her throat as she seemed to relax her whole body.

"Is there anything I can do? You want some water?" Abacus asked. She just shook her head yes. He obliged her and readily brought water to her. She sipped through a straw and braced for the next contraction.

"UGH..." Leslie moaned, her throated noises sounding much like the 'moo' of a cow. Abacus watched helplessly as Leslie's body took on a life of its own.

"Abe..I...need you to...check." Leslie said, her voice soft and wispy from exertion. Abacus looked and found that the baby was already crowning. He told Leslie to bear down with all her might when she felt a contraction. One large push and a cute squishy face was peeking at Abacus. With tears in his eyes, he encouraged Leslie to push again. Two more pushes and Abacus caught a squalling, slippery newborn in his arms. He quickly wrapped the tiny bundle in a warm towel, handing the baby to Leslie as he prepared for the delivery of the second baby. Leslie kept the baby boy close to her body, sharing her body heat with her son. Paramedics entered the bathroom just as other contractions began to intensify. After another strong push, Leslie's daughter made her entrance into the world. After Leslie safely delivered the placenta, the paramedics finished clamping and cutting the cords of both babies. They wrapped her daughter in a heating blanket and snuggled her close to their mother. Leslie smiled as she gazed lovingly at her two bundles of joy. Leslie and the babies were quickly loaded onto a stretcher and rushed off to the hospital.

Chapter 29

The trial had become intense. The prosecutor wasted no time showing proof after proof of Chris's probable guilt. There were times when Mia felt very uncomfortable as she waited for her turn on the stand. She tried her best not to look Chris in the face. But at least once she caught herself staring into his eyes. She could feel the hatred he had for her. She wondered if he ever truly loved her. There had been a time when she loved Chris more than life itself and she would have done anything for him. But those days were long gone. Mia had turned state evidence against Chris in exchange for 10 years in the state penitentiary for women.

When it was Ed's turn to take the stand, he answered the prosecutor's questions and he told the jury everything that had transpired between the four of them after they left the Tiger's night club in downtown Atlanta. When it was time for him to be cross examined Ed knew that Chris's lawyer was going to expose all his darkest secrets and soon the world would know about his sexual addiction. Ed tried his best not to look toward the direction of the cameras and news reporters as he testified.

"Is it true sir that you and your ex-wife are Swingers?" Chris's attorney asked.

"No not really, she only did it once. Leslie really didn't want to swing."

"A yes or no is all we require sir. Have you and your wife ever participated in having sex with other partners as a couple?"

"Yes," Ed mumbled not happy about having his sex life on trial.

"Is it true that you met with Chris on several occasions on business before the night he met your wife?"

"Yes."

"Is it true that you've been diagnosed with a sexual addiction disorder and that you've had multiple affairs?"

"Yes, but what does my sexual issues have to do with him killing Tammy?" Ed blurted out.

"Is it true that Tammy was pregnant with your child and had threatened to tell your wife about the pregnancy?"

"Yes."

"Is it also true that she had already been blackmailing your firm for thousands of dollars, which your firm paid her every month?"

“Yes,” Ed replied.

“Threatening you and your father that she was going to the press with her story and that your wife would find out about your continued infidelities with her and other women despite counseling?" The attorney continued.

Ed paused before answering. "Yes," he mumbled.

“That must have really made you and your father very upset. After all, Edward Sr. worked years to build a good name for his law firm.”

"Yes," Ed frowned.

“Maybe you were so upset that you ordered her killed,” the attorney accused.

“I had nothing to do with her murder!” Ed yelled.

"Did your father tell you how upset he was with your behavior Ed?" The attorney asked as he paced back and forth between the jury and Ed.

"Yes."

"Your father has always gone out of his way to protect you and the firm. Always cleaning up your messes." The attorney accused.

"I don't know what you're talking about." Ed replied trying to figure out where this questioning was headed.

"I don't have any further questions for this witness your honor. I would like to call Edward Johnson Sr. to the stand." The attorney stated as he walked away. Ed stepped down as his father walked up to the podium and was sworn in.

"You must have been really tired of having to clean up after you son," The attorney stated. Edward Sr. started coughing.

" We've discovered that you were so upset that you paid $200,000 to get rid of your son's blackmailer?" The attorney accused dramatically as he turned to face the jury.

"What! No way, that's a lie! He never paid anyone anything!" Ed shouted, jumping to his feet.

"Sit down and be quiet before I charge you with contempt!" The judge ordered. Ed slowly sat down. The attorney smiled as he walked back over to Ed's father and stood in front of him before walking over to the table and picking up stacks of paper and slamming it down on the desk in front of him.

"What if I told you that we took the liberty of checking all your business accounts? It looks like you had two withdraws of $100,000 from your business account. One two weeks before Tammy was murdered and another one the day after she was murdered. What if I also told you that we have an eye witness who's willing to testify that you paid his boss $100,000 to carry out the hit on Tammy?" The attorney asked as he picked the papers back up and walked back toward the jury waving the papers in his hand. A shocked look covered some of the juror's faces.

Mia almost fell out of her chair. She always assumed Chris had been the one to order the hit on Tammy. Never in a million years did she assume Ed's father was involved. Could it be true? Mia thought to herself as she continued to listen to Edward Sr.'s testimony.

Edward Sr. didn't say anything at first. He started coughing again. He pulled a handkerchief from his suit jack and wiped his mouth. He looked at his son with sadness in his eyes as he answered the question.

"Yes," he paused. "I ordered the hit on Tammy. But I never ordered for my son to be framed for her murder nor did I order to have his wife kidnapped. That must have been Chris and Mia," Edward Sr. confessed. The court room erupted as the press scrambled to call in this new bit of information to their higher ups, each wanting to be the first to break the news to the public.

"Quiet in the court!" The judge ordered.

"The tramp was trying to destroy my son and everything I had worked so hard to build. I had to do something!" Ed's father yelled before he started coughing again. Ed sat in disbelief. He couldn't believe what he was hearing. His father had been the one to give the order to have Tammy killed.

When court was dismissed, Ed didn't waste time with niceties, he practically bolted for the door, hoping to avoid any of the press that were sure to hound him about his statements on the witness stand. He ducked out a back-door entrance and mercifully found his rental car with relative ease.

As he drove away from the courthouse his mind wandered back to the first time he'd met Leslie, he wasn't sure why exactly, but he'd been thinking of her often lately.

"Hi." Ed said, hoping the new girl in school wouldn't just blow him off. She looked up and smiled, a polite smile that didn't quite reach her beautiful eyes.

"Hello." Leslie said, noticing the eagerness that practically fell off the guy in waves. She gave him a polite smile and waited. He seemed to be expecting something.

"I don't mean to be too forward, but would you mind if I walk you home. I'll carry your books for you."

Leslie flushed, not quite sure what to say. She'd heard about Ed from the other girls, polite and very cute, but he was a hoe and little bit of a loser. She wondered, all be it shallowly, if being seen with him would help or hurt her reputation.

"Um, sure." Leslie gave in.

Ed was so polite and courteous, opening the door for Leslie's as they walked out of the school building.

"You want to stop at the 'Café on the Corner' on the way home? I'll buy you something." He favored for their exceptional cheesecake. There was, to Ed's mind, nothing that went better with milk than cheesecake.

Ed's day dream went in fast forward motion. He smiled when he thought about the first night they made love. He couldn't bed Leslie as quickly as he had with all his previous lovers. She had been resistant to having sex with him until they were married. She told him she was a virgin and wanted to wait. For some reason the thought of chasing her had excited him.

"You're finally mine." He whispered in Leslie's ear on their wedding night, as he continued to fill her. Her legs wrapped around his waist as he moved his hips back and forth going deep and hard.

"Yes baby, I'm yours, you can have it for life." Leslie yelled out as an orgasm rocked through her body, causing a sensation to spread from her toes to the top of her head.

The sound of someone blowing the horn in the car behind him brought Ed back to the present. He didn't realize that the light had turned green.

"I'm going!" Ed yelled in the review mirror as he turned onto I-20W ramp and headed towards his house. He shivered at the thought of what his father had done. When Ed's father found out that Tammy was pregnant he had exploded. He told Ed that he was being careless and was jeopardizing not only his marriage but also the reputation of the law firm. When Ed's father found out that Tammy had also been blackmailing Ed and the firm for money, his father told Ed not to worry and that he would handle it. Ed assumed that his father was going to pay her off like he had done all the other women. Never in a million years did Ed believe that his father was capable of having someone killed. Ed felt sick to his stomach. He knew his father was going to spend the rest of his life in prison. At that moment, Ed knew that he had to make some drastic life changes. He picked up the phone and called his therapist.

"I need to start going to Sex Addicts Anonymous meetings. Can you set me up with one in my area?" He asked as soon as she answered the phone.

"Sure Ed, once I find one I'll give you a call with the time, date, and location."

"Great."

As Ed was driving, he noticed a church on his way home. He decided to stop and find out about Sunday services. Ed knew that if he was going to make a change in his life, he needed some serious help from the good Lord above.

Chapter 30

Leslie woke to the soft light that filtered in through the windows of her bedroom. It had been nearly four months since she'd given birth rather quickly in that hotel room. She'd loved the experience of having two wonderfully healthy babies and relished every day with them and their father. She smiled as she snuggled closer to Abacus, his long torso the perfect place for her to rest her head. She laid next to him and sigh contentedly. For a minute she didn't notice anything amiss. Her love bubble, as she liked to call it, was so full that she couldn't quite believe how blessed she was. She ran her hand up Abacus's finely sculpted torso, she noticed that his body felt strangely cold. She rested her head against his heart. She couldn't hear his heartbeat. Dread slammed into her with the force of a strong hurricane.

"Abe," Leslie whispered, giving her husband a small shake. He lay still, unmoving, not breathing, "ABE!" Leslie yelled, her voice firm and loud. She shook him forcefully this time, fighting the tears that ran down her cheeks.

Leslie heard the whimpers and startled cries of her new babies and couldn't move to comfort them. The sound of the blood rushing through her system was deafening and the overload of adrenaline made her brave in ways she couldn't fathom.

"ABE!" Leslie was now screaming, she was only barely aware that people were scurrying around her, two maids held her squalling children and someone held her shoulders firmly when all she wanted to do was curl up next to her husband. The tears fell freely now, sobs racked her body and she trembled uncontrollably. She watched through unseeing eyes as someone called the police and ambulance. Time seemed to stand still as she watched the paramedics attend to Abacus. She refused to leave his side, holding his hand in a fierce grip, willing him to breathe and wake up.

They loaded Abacus's body onto the gurney as a paramedic came over to talk with her, his face grim.

"Ma'am, I'm very sorry, but your husband has passed away." NO! Her mind screamed over and over again. She couldn't, absolutely couldn't lose him! Her quiet sobs became gut wrenching moans of grief, confusion, anger, and denial.

She didn't attend to her babies, so consumed by her grief that she couldn't see past a minute at a time. She was only slightly aware that someone brought her soup that she didn't eat. She didn't drink or sleep. She kept calling for him, wondering why he refused to answer. Finally, exhaustion won and she fell into a fitful, angry sleep.

"ABE! Answer me damn it!" Leslie yelled, jerking awake with a startled cry. She automatically reached for Abe, finding his side of the bed empty, she once again gave in to the tears that seemed to control her with every breath she took. She heard one of her babies stir. As if on autopilot, Leslie got up to see about her.

"Hello sweet girl." Leslie cooed to her daughter as she changed her diaper. She carried her daughter over to the bed. Propping herself up on a pillow, she allowed her daughter to nurse until she fell back into a deep sleep. She kissed her sweet little girl on the forehead and placed her back in the crib alongside her brother. Then with a soft sob she sank to the floor and cried out all her sorrow, whispering to her babies just how much she missed their father.

The next morning Leslie pulled herself into the shower, still on autopilot, she somehow managed to fumble through the process of washing up. She brushed her teeth and hair and then dressed in a set of Abacus's sweat pants and a white T-shirt. They still held his smell and her tears fell freely. Her soft sobs echoed throughout her room and she screamed out all her anguish and anger.

"I HATE YOU ABACUS!" Leslie sobbed, "I HATE YOU FOR LEAVING ME!" Leslie sank onto the bed and beat the pillows beneath her head, feeling the grief and anger pour out of her like molten liquid. Softer now, she told Abacus about all the things she'd wanted to share with him.

"I can't do this alone Abe! I'm not strong enough without you. I...I don't have it in me." Wisps of conversations she'd shared with Abe came back to her as she cried, "You are the bravest, most amazing woman I've ever known Leslie. I'm the one who needs you." She could hear him saying.

Leslie walked around her bedroom like a zombie as she tried to prepare for the funeral and burial of her husband. The doctor said Abe had an enlarged heart and that at some point during the night it had stopped beating. Leslie felt a small bit of comfort in knowing that he had felt no pain and died peacefully in her arms. She stared at the plain black dress the servants had laid out for her. She just couldn't seem to bring herself to put the dress on. Suddenly there was a brief knock on the door before Aunt Agatha peeked her head inside the room.

"Are you okay honey? "Agatha asked as she walked into the room slowly closing the door behind her. Agatha had been Abacus's favorite aunt. Abacus told Leslie that after his mother had died from childbirth, Agatha had helped raise him and his brothers in the palace. As soon as Leslie saw Agatha walk towards her, she couldn't contain the tears.

"Why did he have to leave us?" Leslie sobbed as Agatha embraced her. Agatha walked Leslie over to the bed and sat down.

"I know it hurts child. I know the pain of losing a loved one. "Agatha said as she softly stroked Leslie's hair. "I know how hard this must be for you. But you must be strong child. You must be strong for the kingdom. Everyone is looking for you to help them get through this."

"I'm not set out for this life Aunt Agatha, I don't know what to say to these people. All I know is that the man I loved, and the father of my children is dead." Leslie said as she lowered her head. Aunt Agatha put her hand under Leslie's chin and lifted her head so that she could look into her eyes.

"You are stronger than you give yourself credit for. Don't worry, I'll be there with you. Now come on so that you can get dressed." Aunt Agatha said as she stood up and picked the dress off the bed and held it out for Leslie. Leslie stared at Agatha for what seemed like an eternity before she took the dress from her and walked into the bathroom.

For more than a month Leslie went through the motions of living, without participating. She watched over her babies, fed them, bathed them, talked gently with them during their 'tummy time' or during meals. But her eyes held none of the spark that Abacus had so loved about her. She was a human shell. Pain and sorrow were holding her soul and spirit prisoner.

"Your Highness?" Gertrude, the maid gently pried, one afternoon about two months after Abe's passing. Leslie looked up, her eyes no longer hollowed out, but still not shining the way they had with Abe, "I was wondering if you could go with me to the market today. I want to make the twins an outfit and would like their mother's opinion of the fabric." Leslie finally lamented and packing up her two babies, she went to the market with her maid.

The market was a lively place, full of the colors and brightness of life. It teemed with the echoes of cat calls and the shouts of profits and losses. Leslie walked through it without noticing, numb to the world around her and still in a state of shock and grief. She could sense the whispering around her, she barely noticed the sideways glances that came her way as she meandered through the marketplace.

Gertrude chattered lively as she grabbed fresh fruit, fresh vegetables, and new linens. She had a mind to make the babies a set of spring clothes and was chomping at the bit to get the cook to bake a rhubarb pie. Leslie would smile whenever she mentioned her ideas, but that smile never reached her eyes. And the fight to keep her composure was almost more than she could bear.

After what seemed like an eternity, Leslie and Gertrude returned to the palace. Leslie left the babies with the nanny and Gertrude in the capable hands of Bertha, the cook, and wandered the palace grounds. She eventually found her way to Abacus's grave. She placed a bouquet of handpicked flowers at his headstone, and then sat down to pour out her heart, again.

"You'd be so enamored with our children, Abe." Leslie said, the tears falling easily off her cheeks. "I can't believe how much they've grown.

They're already squabbling with each other about who gets which bite of food." Despite her poor mood Leslie chuckled. She could just imagine Abacus's exasperation when the twins threw their food on the floor or at each other. He had been a strict man on organization and their two little minions would have ruined all that hard work. Leslie spent another hour or so talking to Abacus, the only source of healing she seemed to be able to find. And even though her heart still ached, she felt lighter inside than she had in a long time.

Chapter 31

Ed walked into his house and threw the pamphlets from his Sex Anonymous meeting on the kitchen counter. He walked into the living room just in time to hear Leslie leaving a message on his answering machine. He threw his keys on the table and ran over to the phone.

"Hello Ed, this is Leslie. I..." Ed grabbed the phone interrupting Leslie in mid-sentence.

"Leslie, how are you baby?" Ed asked smiling.

"Fine," Leslie whispered into the phone trying not to let the tears begin again.

"Baby, what's wrong?" Ed asked as he sat down on his couch. He could tell something was bothering her.

"My husband is dead," Leslie whispered in the phone.

"Dead? How, when?" Ed asked in shock.

“He had a heart attack about three months ago.” Leslie couldn’t stop the tears from falling down her face. Ed could hear her sniffles through the phone.

“Oh, baby don’t cry. I’m so sorry to hear that.” A small piece of him hated hearing her call another man her husband. In his heart, she was still his wife.

“I just feel so lost over here without him.” Leslie whispered.

“Why don’t you come back to the States?”

“I don’t know, I have the twins and I’m just not sure.”

“Well, you know your family would help you with the babies and so would I. You could even stay at the house if you want. After all, this house still belongs to you too.” Ed replied secretly praying that she would say yes.

“I do miss my family. Being here is just making me more depressed. Everything reminds me of him. I’ll think about it. Listen I have to go, I hear one of the twins crying. I’ll call you later.”

“Okay, I’m always here if you need to talk.” Ed said before hearing the line go dead. He sat on the couch in silence staring out the front window as he thought about the possibility of Leslie coming back to the US and coming home to him.

Leslie spent a week going back and forth about what she should do. Should she go home? She would love to see her family. Was she really ready to see Ed? What about leaving Abe? Who was she kidding, he was dead.

Finally, after a week of busy days and near sleepless nights, she came to a hard decision. She called a meeting with her top staff and Abacus's younger brother Maximus. Her fingers nervously twisted her handkerchief as she waited to inform them that she was passing the throne on to him and returning to America.

"Thank you for coming on such short notice Max." Leslie said as she greeted Abacus's baby brother with the traditional kiss on each cheek. He grabbed her in a hard hug.

"Anything for you." Max said, grinning. Leslie could still see the sadness in his eyes because it mirrored exactly how she felt.

"Alright everyone!" Leslie's voice carried over her audience and they all politely bowed and took their seats, “First of all thank-you for making this meeting, even though it's last minute! I wanted to express how grateful I am to everyone here for their support and encouragement after Abe's passing.

When the crown passed down to me I felt such a heavy burden for our people and I was terrified of doing something wrong. All of you helped me to make sure I didn't.” Tears filled Leslie's eye, but she continued knowing that Abe would be proud of her,

“Over the last week I've been struggling with a hard decision, and I've finally made up my mind. I've decided to pass the throne over to Max. When Abe passed away I lost such an intensely vital part of myself that I no longer feel it is right for me to hold the throne. Within the next week I will be leaving, me and the children will be returning to my home in America.”

Leslie ignored the audible gasp and trudged along,

“I understand that there is a need for some transitional time, so I've allotted one month's time from the end of next week for that. If within that one-month period, Max or the board feels that it isn't a job that he can handle, I will return and figure out a new replacement. However, once the one month is up neither Max nor you may contact me concerning the Kingship. I would however love to get news of my staff and all of you, on how things are doing! I will send correspondence often with updates on the twins'. And when they are old enough, and Max has gotten long in his loafers, I will tell them of their heritage and their right by birth to this throne and it's amazing people!"

Cheers went up when Leslie finished speaking. Leslie spent time amongst her staff, hugs and traditional kisses were exchanged. For the first time Leslie felt as if she could breathe again. Max stayed close by her side, offering his own congratulations on a well delivered resignation. He spent the next week at the palace working closely with Leslie and members of her staff to acquaint himself with being King.

"I can't believe so much is required!" Max said, running a hand through his thick black hair. Leslie hadn't missed the family resemblance.

"It is definitely a lot to take in." Leslie said, reaching for her coffee. She yawned and rubbed her tired eyes. The twins had been asleep for quite a while and she groaned when she looked at the time, "Ugh, there's still so much to do and I feel run down already." Max looked at her then, and noticed the shadows under her eyes, and the sadness that marred her otherwise perfect complexion.

"Feel like a nightcap?" Max asked, hoping to cheer up a little. He knew some of her pain, because there wasn't a day that went by that he didn't miss his brother. He poured three stiff fingers of brandy and handed her the glass. She smiled and sipped it slowly, enjoying the little burn in her belly. They finished their drinks with little conversation between them. She smiled, kissed Max on the cheek, and said goodnight.

By weeks end Leslie was starting to feel excited about finishing up the last of the transition to Max and getting ready to fly back to America. She smiled sadly as she looked around her bedroom. She'd been ecstatic here with Abe, content with him and the babies; but now it didn't feel like home anymore. America would always be that pillar for her. And that's where she needed to be, where she wanted to raise her children. She sent a quick message to Ed, letting him know that she'd be back in Atlanta by the next afternoon.

The next day, Max accompanied Leslie and the twins to the airport.

"Thank you for everything you've done for us since we lost Abe." Leslie said, giving Max a hug.

"I'll write often and send pictures of the twins. You'll come to see us in America, won't you Max?"

"Yes of course! You're not getting rid of me that easily," he chuckled. "I'll try to make yearly visits to the US, I promise," Max reassured her. He spent a few minutes loving on his niece and nephew before he watched Leslie board the aircraft with the twins.

After getting situated in her seat, Leslie took a deep breath as the airplane took off. She stared out the window as the airplane ascended into the clouds. So much had happened over the last three years. A tinge of sadness touched her heart when she thought about Abe. She glanced down at her twins and smiled. Her smile faded as her thoughts turned to Ed. He sounded so excited about her and the twins returning to America. She had to admit that something in his voice seemed different. Maybe he has changed, Leslie thought to herself.

Chapter 32

Leslie stepped off the plane in Atlanta holding one twin in each arm. She stood in the corridor with the other passengers and waited for her twin's stroller to be taken off the plane. Ed and her family were waiting for her in the baggage claim. Leslie had to admit that if felt kind of weird being back in America. When the airport baggage handler placed her stroller in the aisle she had to place both the babies on the floor so that she could open the stroller. Once she had them both fastened in she smiled, the twins were looking more and more like Abe every day. She exhaled deeply before grabbing the handle of the stroller and pushing it down the aisle towards the baggage claim. As she got closer to the baggage claim carousel, she saw her parents and Ed waving at her as they began walking in her direction with smiles on their faces. Her father reached her first.

"Oh, baby, we missed you so much." Her father said as he hugged her joined a few seconds later by her mother who joined in on the hug. As they released her they began doting on their grandchildren as Ed walked up to her and hugged.

He smelled so good. Leslie felt something inside of her leap as Ed embraced her, something she had not expected to feel.

"I missed you too." Ed said as he pulled away.

Leslie spent her first week back in America settling into her new apartment. She could have afforded an elaborate home on the stipend she received from Abacus's allowance but decided to rent an apartment instead. She paid the rent six months in advance and stashed the rest of the money in a savings account. She knew that at some point the cash flow would end, as Max took over the kingdom. And even though he'd promised to continue to send support for his niece and nephew, she wasn't about to hold him to it. Soon she'd have to find a job, the thought excited her.

She was startled one afternoon when her phone rang.

"Hello?" Leslie said, her voice overly bright from the momentary shock.

“Les?” Ed said, his voice husky and quiet.

“Oh. Hi Ed.” Leslie said, a little unsure of where to take the conversation.

“I was wondering if you'd mind if I took you and your little ones to the park? We could pick up lunch and stroll them through the trails.” Leslie bit her bottom lip in contemplation. There was a part of her that desperately needed companionship, friendship, and love; but she knew Ed and was uncertain he could provide any of those without the lies and deceit and other women, he so often wanted to throw into the mix.

“Um, sure,” Leslie said, finally conceding that a trip to the park was harmless and that it'd do her and the babies good to get out of the house. She bundled them up, packed extra diapers, wet wipes, food, and clothes into their diaper bag, and when Ed came up the drive promptly at 2p.m., they were all ready to go.

“Hi Leslie.” Ed said, feeling the strong stir of desire, despite the fact that she held the hand of a toddler in each hand. She looked better than he'd ever seen her, and the smile she gave him went straight to his heart. He offered to take one of the toddlers, and the diaper bags, helping her situate the carriers into his sedan while she chatted about how good it felt to finally be settling back into life in America.

"I honestly didn't realize how much I missed home. Don't get me wrong, I loved it over there. It was quite an experience being "queen", but in the end it wasn't for me." Ed held Leslie's door for her and shut it securely before walking around to the driver's side. He waited for her to buckle her seat belt before he started the engine and pulled slowly from her inclined driveway.

"So, you're settling in well?" Ed asked, glancing at Leslie. She was staring out the window at the landscape, where spring was slowly appearing.

"We are, it took a little adjusting for the twins, but I think they're doing well now." Leslie said. Ed didn't mention it, mainly because he wasn't sure how to say it without sounding like a prick, but Leslie was different. She looked the same, sounded the same even, but she carried herself with such a fierce sense of confidence he hadn't remembered about her before she'd been kidnapped. He wasn't ready to admit how much that turned him on.

They spent the afternoon at the park, sitting on a blanket, watching the twins play. Leslie had to admit that she hadn't expected Ed to be so great with the twins.

"I've been going to Sex Alcoholics Anonymous meetings every week for the last few months. I also attend church every Sunday. I'm thinking about becoming an usher. Maybe you can attend church with me one Sunday." He said smiling. This surprised Leslie because Ed had never been religious.

"Sure," she said as she handed a sippy cup to her son. She wasn't ready for anything meaningful yet, but it was nice to talk with someone other than her parents or the babies. And she couldn't help noticing how Ed seemed genuinely interested in, not only how she was doing, but how the twins were as well.

Once they decided to leave, Ed helped Leslie tote the twins back to the car and buckle them into their carriers.

"I know this may be too soon, and it's okay if it is. I just, um," he stuttered. "I was wondering if I could take you and the twins to dinner sometime. I'm not sure what they can eat, but it'd be nice to see you more often. And them too of course." Ed said as he helped her get the twins out of the car. Leslie smiled, she'd never imagined that

Ed would stammer trying to ask her out. Even that first time so long ago, he'd been full of quiet, arrogance.

"I'd enjoy that Ed. I must admit that you exceeded my expectations today. Thank you for a great afternoon." Leslie said. They made small talk for another few minutes and then Ed left. He smiled and began whistling as he got behind the wheel of his dark green Cadillac CTS and backed out of her driveway to head home.

EPILOGUE

Over the next year, Ed and Leslie began spending more and more time together. They took the twins to the park almost every weekend and enjoyed dinner dates out at local restaurants. They had begun rebuilding a friendship that had been missing from their marriage. Leslie accompanied Ed whenever he went to Jackson State Prison to visit his father. She even allowed the twins to go a few times. Ed's father was always delighted when he saw the twins.

Ed continued to go to counseling for his nymphomania and was also in group therapy to help him deal with his childhood issues and with his father's incarceration. Ed supported Leslie's decision to press charges against Chris for kidnapping. Ed barely hid his smile when Chris cried like a little bitch, as the judge sentenced him to two life terms in prison.

It took a long time for Ed to fully regain Leslie's trust. But eventually his patience, prayers, and persistence paid off. Three years after Leslie returned to America, Ed and Leslie remarried. He had grown to love her twins, they lovingly called him daddy. When Leslie discovered that she was pregnant, Ed had been frightened that she wouldn't carry the baby full term. But after a wonderful pregnancy without complications, Maria Abagail Johnson was born. Ed and Leslie continued to attend church on a regular basis and even began a marriage ministry, helping other couples who were planning to get married, on the verge of divorce, or who wanted to reunite with their ex-spouses. Every time Leslie and Ed shared their unique story with other couples, they laughed at the reaction they received. No one could believe that after all they had gone through, that Ed and Leslie were able to love again, forgive each other, and get remarried. Leslie and Ed loved to end each marriage counseling session with their favorite quote.

"With God, All Things Are Possible."

THE END

Book Discussion

1. Did the ending surprise you?

2. If you were Leslie, do you think you could have forgiven Ed? How did you feel about Ed and Mia's relationship?

3. If you were Ed, do you think you could have accepted Leslie's children? How did you feel about Leslie and Abacus's relationship?

____

____

____

____

____

____

____

____

____

____

____

____

____

____

____

____

____

____

____

____

____

4. How did you feel about Chris and Mia's relationship?

____

____

____

____

____

____

____

____

____

____

____

____

____

____

____

____

____

____

____

____

____

____

____

____

5. How did you feel about Leslie and Chris's relationship?

6. What did you like most about Swingerz?

6. What did you like least about Swingerz?

7. If you could have written the ending, how would you have liked for the book to end?

8. How far would you go to save your marriage? Do you think you could have forgiven Ed?

10. What has someone done to you that you need to forgive them for? Do they know that they hurt you?

11. What have you done to someone that you want them to forgive you for? Have you acknowledged that you hurt them? Have you apologized?

12. How did you feel when Ed went to church, asked for forgiveness, and began taking steps toward changing his life? Do you believe in the power of prayer? Yes/No/ and why?

Author's Note

I must declare to anyone who may be at a crossroad in their life, going through storms in their life, or looking for answers concerning their life, that "God is Not Deaf".

The Lord heard you the first time you prayed and immediately dispatched angels to the scene. While you're waiting for an answer from God or a change in your situation, you must continue to trust God and hold on to your faith.

He knows what's best for you. He has promised that He will never leave your nor forsake you. He will lead and guide you.

I'm learning that believing in God and trusting in God are two very different things. It's possible to believe in the power of God but still not trust in Him to change your situation. I know you were not expecting these last words, but it's what I was led to say.

I hope you enjoyed reading Swingerz...Be blessed and be on the lookout for my next book "The Symbol". Please check out my trilogy series; This Can't Be Love, This Can't Be Love2, and Ladies Delight.
www.patriciagoinsbooks.com.

Peace & Love,

Patricia M. Goins

Made in the USA
Columbia, SC
20 August 2024